THE
EMBERS
READER

30 Short Tales by Gerald Bosacker

THE AUTHOR,

Gerald Bosacker is a prolific poet and tale-teller who is minimally discovered by the paying public, but lavishly displayed, pro bono on the internet. Existing by charging tasting-fees for food and 'comfort-rating' fee from his landlord. Survival techniques acquired as a poverty-plagued writer subjected to 'reading-fees' for his literary contributions. Long ago while student at the University of Minnesota, he was sidetracked from his journalism study by hunger and other economic needs, forcing full-time work.

Bosacker became a printer, then a salesman, who successfully migrated upward, propelled by serendipity coupled with his love and application of fiction, to become V.P. of Sales for a moderately successful international company. Promoted beyond his ambition and capability, Bosacker jumped at the chance for early retirement. Now living among his aging peers in a Florida retirement community, he has resumed his first love, weaving words into prize winning poetry and surprising tales that borrow heavily from the fascinating people dealt with in his travels.

DIRECTORY

Printed in the USA, for EmberS Press, SAN: 255-5425
ISBN # 0-9743640-1-0

DEDICATION
Although all of the characters depicted in this collection of short
stories are fictional, and only suggested by persons the author met
in his travels, the real inspiration and support are quite identifiable.
Without the forbearance, encouragement, andAnd suggestions of
my wife, Jacky, son John and daughter Jill Courtney, these pages
would be blank.

A JURY OF ONE

Paul's over-filled bladder forced him awake and the brown taste on his tongue accused him of pagan debauchery the night before, doubling his discomfiture. He could not open his sleep encrusted eyes, and he could not mobilize his hands seemingly attached to his hairy belly. The curse his larynx formed refused to open his lips, and the effort pulled on every hair of his moustache, which now seemed to be rooted to his lower lip and chin. Someone was clumsily manipulating his pee hardened penis. Who could it be? Did he come home alone? Was this a nightmare? He fervently hoped this was the start of an adventure with someone who, depraved like him, treasured anonymity and Paul shivered with anticipation.

"Oh good, you're awake, Paul. Don't struggle, just lie back and enjoy the moment. I certainly remember how much you enjoy kinky sex."

"Hmmph, arumph frump," He said, demanding to know who was there and why. He didn't remember bringing anyone home with him and seldom succeeded in recruiting an overnight guest.

"I'm so hurt that you don't remember me. Maybe that's because the last time we frolicked, we never finished, did we?"

Well, that didn't narrow it down. A lot of his past romantic adventures had ended prematurely. The voice was indistinct, and could be anyone of the many girls he had seized and forcibly loved. "Ooom, ummmph," He mumbled painfully and resisted trying to say more.

"Don't fight, Paul. Remember, that's what you told me. I want to make sure you enjoy this every bit as much as I did."

His hands stayed firmly clasped together as if his fingers had lost separate identities and had rooted to his paunch. Why?

"I couldn't find the duct tape you used on me, Paul. I had to improvise with the super glue I brought. I hope you don't mind me improvising on your technique."

Paul tried swinging his feet to the floor, preparing to run blindly for the door, even if he did not know how he would open it without hands.

"Don't struggle, Paul. I took the liberty of fastening your feet to the foot board of your bed. You can't run out on me, Paul. I need to return the pleasures you bestowed on me. I promise this adventure will last a long time."

Paul clenched his teeth. It hurt to try opening his lips. He did not have strength to unclench his eyelids, as the lashes stayed firmly enmeshed, as if glued. Could his tormentor be that little mousey thing with the nasal whimper Paul had tricked into meeting him for house tour, last week? That wimpy little creature had submitted too quickly, with almost no struggle. Just plaintively begging to first him and then her God. His captor's voice was much stronger but there was a strong similarity.

"Remember how I begged you to use a condom, at least? Well I brought a whole package, and I will fasten them securely with super glue so they will never come off. Funny stuff, super glue. They even use it in place of stitches in the operating room. We don't want you to spread your seed or diseases, do we?"

Her manipulations of his throbbing sex organ did not evoke pleasure. Paul strained, trying to empty his bladder, hoping to explode the latex encasing his swollen phallus but the glue had already set, sealing his urethra shut. The pushing pain of his bladder was unbearable.

"I have to go, Paul. I have an appointment to show that house you were interested in. You know, with the scratchy carpeting. I will check back in a few days to see how you are doing....maybe."

"Umppph, mummmmph," he managed, but no one would know he was begging forgiveness and pleading for mercy. He tried a silent prayer to the same god his victim had tried, but recalled it had not rescued her from his demands. Minutes later, Paul heard the door slam, but that only signaled the exit of his tormentor. Now, Paul remembered clearly how vehemently that chubby and submissive realtor, had promised revenge. God, how he wished he could forget or undo that one unappreciated stolen adventure. Doomed to slowly and painfully drown in his own pee, Paul resolved to never again rape a woman, no matter how badly they deserved or wanted it to happen.

WHY ARGUE

Why don't you let good manners rule,

        politely differ, never fight.

We must not argue with a fool,

        always certain that he is right.

When you suspect you might be wrong,

        you try to win by loudest voice.

Only donkeys are more headstrong,

        so be an Ass, if that's your choice.

When we dare try to voice our view,

        you interrupt, and that's so rude.

That's why we hate to talk with you,

        and you deserve that solitude.

ALIEN DETECTOR

He was the most bland and non-descript man I had ever met, and yet, I remember his face as well as my own. I am tall, dark and some eager or desperate women would think me handsome. I remembered him as sort of blonde and almost stocky. No special details to note, his features all being sort of average, like an alien interloper would assume. I nicknamed him X. His eyes, when I caught him looking at me, were of a color not definable, like deep water, dependent on the reflected image. You could only guess at what he observed or if he saw anything at all. I remember staring at his eyes, then looking to see if he carried a white cane. X was difficult to describe, yet I will never forget him.

I do not remember what X wore so he must have been dressed like all the other commuters on the Sylvan Park Metro Line. He sat directly across from me and I am sure he exited at the Elm Street Park exit, but I was in a hurry and rushed off, while he sat motionless. As I walked down the outside of the stopped car toward the steps, I saw through the window that X had moved or had exited, too. Curious, I stopped at the water fountain and stealthily observed each passerby, but did not see him. I did sense his presence and knew X was following me.

I did not favor walking the frightening four blocks to my apartment through poorly lit streets of a dangerous neighborhood in the dusk of December with someone dogging my steps. Cautiously, I crossed to the other side of the transit stop and waited for the downtown run. No one seemed to be waiting for me and I had nothing but the sure mediocrity of television planned for the evening, so a diversionary trip seemed wise. Especially, because the briefcase I carried contained my only working copy of the Bozo Electron Detector.

This miraculous breakthrough, I first conceived while still a Doctoral candidate in Physics at Michigan State. That ended with great embarrassment. Later, I had a more spare time while teaching at the local Urban Community College and continued development of the electron sensor. I did so on the quiet, working in their well equipped laboratory nights, and their lack of awareness of my invention's importance caused an abrupt dismissal again. While unemployed, again, I worked on the project with my own meager funds. My field testing succeeded and I knew that it would rock the world when I published my discoveries.

Groping in my pocket, I found another token, and soon I heard the shrill whistle and oncoming rumble of the downtown bound Express 314, and almost on its appointed 6:33 schedule. I had used this train many times, while on the Community College faculty, albeit probationary. It did allow me clandestine access to their well equipped electronic labs, with the needed esoteric and expensive electronic tools I could not afford. If my jealous Teaching Assistant had not reported a little bit of unauthorized night-time usage of the laboratory, I would have been contentedly teaching numb nuts too dense to gain admittance to a real school, but the work on my detector was done, except for field testing.

Downtown traffic was light this early and only two young people and one yong and garish professional lady of the night, waited on the platform. I hesitated until the last moment before boarding and did not see X, my mystery stalker.

Still relatively flush with money from my last severance settlement, I decided to splurge on dinner at an Indian Restaurant, I had just discovered and liked because they did vegetables in a most savory manner. I would try scanning the downtown evening pedestrian traffic with my detector if the batteries still held sufficient charge. I could try an hour in front of WBBN studio hoping to catch their newscasters, and show them my Bozo Electronics Detector. I would have to scan them first, as I don't want to let any already infiltrated aliens know that my invention detects their internal circuitry.

The dinner was great although I panicked when I thought I tasted meat in the spiced peas. That would be typical of the Alien's poisoning tactics, and signify that the they were already aware of my electronic circuitry detecting ability. I couldn't scan for that give-a-way alien circuitry in any of the kitchen staff because my batteries failed, and it could be the taste of the cumin fooling me. With no reason to remain downtown if I couldn't test or demonstrate my gadget's alien detecting ability so I went home. I saw no sign of my shadow, but X was there.

The next morning, batteries charged and carrying two sets of spares, I left for the city with the commuters on the morning seven-ten. There X sat, across from me, ignoring my stares. When we reached Central, he left so I followed him. On fourth street, he unlocked and entered a barber shop, then snuck through a curtained door to the back room. Switching on my detector, I entered the shop quietly. I had the very sensitive but heavy ceramic cone antenna unit up in front of me, like a skeet shooter bracing to shoot. It detected a strong signal, when he came back almost bumping the detector cone. My BED's power meter read full signal transmitting and left no doubt that X was an alien.

Sure, he wore a barber's apron and I would have thought him such, if didn't have my detector pointed at his head. He tried to confuse me, offering me his money and wallet, like he thought me a common thief. Aliens are very clever! I was unarmed and worried that he would de-energize me so I hit him with the heavy cone end of my alien detector very hard, again and again. I saw a miniature electronic circuitry unit pop out of his bleeding ear, and I knew I had destroyed another alien invader. You tell me that I killed an innocent but near deaf barber and all the circuitry I detected was only remnants of his smashed hearing aid. Well, maybe. And maybe you are detectives as you claim and not aliens but if you'll just let me have my detector, I can tell for sure.

ALTHEA'S WAY

The cars exiting Interstate 99 moved fast and were beyond me before their drivers could see my outstretched thumb. Stalled for an hour, I vainly sought pity or a traveler needing company to stay awake. Traffic seemed too intent on merging with the steady stream of cars speeding south on toward San Diego or beyond to the Mexican border. Leaving my last ride at this busy junction rather than in Riverside where ride chances were better, was foolish, and maybe catastrophic.

. This intersection was well lit and my dress whites were still clean and almost unwrinkled but it would soon be dark and my shore leave expired at tomorrow's reveille. Hitchhiking had not been a planned part of my gambling trip to Las Vegas nor had I planned on losing my last twenty on the craps table no pass line.

The lonely five dollar bill and lose change in my pockets would keep me in cigarettes and coffee or bus fare from the outskirts of San Diego to my ship's dock. Not both, and those outskirts could be hours away. I had violated the gamblers most sacred rule, not holding back enough money for the fare home.

Rides had been good until then, all drivers expecting only conversation, which I dutifully supplied, with little exaggeration or embellishment. My role as a Pharmacist Mate, serving on a Destroyer in the South China Sea did not provide much grist for glory. Saving Vietnamese boat people fleeing the Viet Cong had been exciting and humane, if not heroic.

Passing cars seemed totally unconcerned over my plight and were probably driven by Apeace at any cost" liberals who would only stop if I were wearing black pajamas. Risking injury, I edged closer to the traffic lane, my thumb extended into the scorning traffic, sure that slight injury was preferable to total indifference.

Eventually, I saw a slow-moving car and what a beauty. A pristine, twenty-year old Buick Convertible, massive and shiny, passing slowly, top down, allowing me a good look at the attractive gray-haired lady driver. She was obviously assessing my latent peril or innocence, and I must have passed inspection. Her beautiful Buick oozed to a stop eighty feet down the road, over on the shoulder, almost into the ditch. I sprinted for the car, and with reassuring politeness, said, "Thanks for stopping, Ma'am. I am really grateful!"

"You're in a bad place to get a ride, young man, and that's why I stopped. I'm not going far, just 'exorcizing' this old monster, but I can get you on down to where the slower moving traffic will be far less suspicious and much more disposed to stop," she said, smiling so broadly that her facial wrinkles disappeared, leaving her much prettier and younger than I suspected her to be. A faint but exciting wisp of lilac blended with the smell of well tended leather sweetened the air.

We rode along in silence for quite a while, analyzing each other surreptitiously, and when assured and confident, she continued, "Actually, I was hoping you'd be friendly or hungry enough to have dinner with me. I hate eating alone when I'm driving with no place to go. You don't look psychotic or dangerous. Are you?"

"Oh no, Ma'am, I'm just grateful for the ride and good company. I really dig your car. I love older things," I blurted, hoping she didn't think that included her. She stared straight ahead, maybe puzzled, so I began again, "I would love to treat you to dinner but I blew my wad in Las Vegas, and have to be ship-side in the morning."

"Dear Boy, I'm almost old enough to be your mother and only thinking of your welfare," she said, with just a hint of understatement. Then she invitingly said, "I wouldn't want you to starve in the brig, or stop growing.. You just let me do the planning, and you will get to your boat before they know you're gone." I guessed she was more than old enough to be my mother though she was slim, attractive and very well dressed, as if going to a party. She had been a very beautiful woman and that quality still graced her face, while her body looked as well preserved as that of her magnificent car.

Reassured, I said, "You're the captain of this crew, Ma'am and I haven't had a prettier captain or sailed in a nicer boat! Your wish is my command!" I liked my response, thinking it worthy of inclusion in the book I would someday write and looked for some sign of appreciation. She was apparently too busy crossing traffic lanes to appreciate good dialogue. Now traveling slower on the outside lane, I worried she was dropping me there for my brashness.

I worried more when she abruptly pulled off the interstate, onto a service road. We entered the parking lot of small supper club with one very small neon sign displaying, 'The Pirate"s Mess'. This would not be a good place to catch another ride! "My name is Althea and this is my favorite place, but I never stop to eat if I'm alone. After our dinner I'll make sure that you're in San Diego with an hour to spare! I'll even let you drive Greg's damned old sleeze-buggy. You could probably pick up a couple of young and willing females like he always did."

That invitation eased my concerns, although she seemed nervous, almost like she was playing a role and had a little stage fright. I wondered if, Althea was even her real name. No longer worried about catching a ride and comfortably seated, I asked, "Who is this Greg who doesn't appreciate what a great babe he's got. I think you're far prettier than most young girls I meet. Greg must be a real dummy." I knew I sounded funny and was stammering, so I excused myself without waiting for her answer and needed to ponder on this perplexing situation.

Inside, Althea had ordered double Manhattans, while I, for what had seemed a lifetime, finally drained my bladder. A consequence of spending almost two hours stalled where there were no public utilities but too much traffic to use the weeds. When I returned to our table she was slowly sipping on her drink while she explained, "Greg is my husband. We'd been married five years when his bachelor uncle died leaving Greg a small estate big enough to allow me to quit my job at the bank and start having babies. Greg selfishly spent it all on himself. The first thing he bought was that damned Roadmaster Convertible, paying almost half as much as he earned in a year, selling shoes. He was always selfish, and probably didn't want to share any thing with children. That was the day I stopped loving him. After getting the car, he worked later and later, and went to more and more night meetings. As selfish as he was, he would generously share his lovemaking with others and he worked very hard at that. Whenever the phone rang, Greg would run to be first to answer the phone. Over-hearing his cryptic conversation, I would know it was just some babe he had met cruising in his convertible. I disliked Greg but I hated that car! Soon, he didn't even try to fool me, insulting both me and my intelligence. I rejoiced when his chasing finally ended."

I had finished my manhattan, and somehow another had been ordered. It was a strong but pleasant tasting mix I had never had before but would not dare have another. Dinner was delicious. I did not want to be late for roll call or risk Navy discipline, I fished for the right words to speed our exit, "So where is Greg and why isn't he driving his Buick, and having dinner with you? I understand your anger, but why did his roaming stop?"

"As soon as we've finished our desserts, I'll take you to Greg, you'll love him," she whispered while reaching across the small table to gently hold my hand. Her nervousness was gone...not totally gone, for now the nervousness was mine. I could feel my cheeks flushing while she brashly continued, "Because of your drinks, I'd like you to stay with us, resting a little while, then we can drive to your ship. I will enjoy the ride. We only live a few miles from here. There you'll meet Greg and understand why each weekend I park my little VW Rabbit and drive this big old Buick."

I agreed to her plan because of sudden and surprising lustful hopes, not the justifiable curiosity created by her sad story. The delicious dinner, the relieving of my worry about overstaying my pass, the emerging beauty of my host and all accelerated by the mellowing whiskey had made me ripe for any adventure that might happen.

Althea chose her favorite dessert, a triple chocolate confection called 'Death by Chocolate' and I eagerly agreed to sample what ever was her choice.

The desserts when brought were mammoth and I watched in fascination as Althea ravenously gobbled hers as if we had not just finished huge sea-food dinners. Althea, licked her chocolate coated lips and slowly let a spoonful of the confection melt on her tongue. Looking down at her vanishing dessert, she said, "Chocolate tastes so good but it's always gone too quickly. No matter how much I am given, I always wish for more."

Whiskey brave, I recklessly replied, "Yep, the best treats are those that get bigger as you eat them"

Althea naively started some non-sequitur, then blushed and spluttered, "Good point! I think it's time to go now," abandoning the few morsels remaining in her dish, while I was only half done.

When we were outside in the parking lot, I was still worrying that I had been too rash so was reluctant to chance any action not invited. Yet, I dared to casually brush my lips against her neck, as I opened her car door, helping her enter. Her hand fell on mine, and she gave it a hot and reassuring squeeze. I wondered whether she would stop on the way home, and asked, "When is Greg expecting you home?"

"Have patience, sweetie! He is used to waiting," she said then resumed driving in silence, and I did not know what I would say when I would meet her Greg. I knew my must was evident but maybe we would stop and attend to that, first. Althea had to be aware of my lust as I could smell my pheremones...or was it hers?

She did not stop and shortly Althea turned into a long shadowy driveway leading to a darkened Rambler that was somewhat unusually shaped. It had a ramp across the front that starkly contrasted with the house's lines. Only the front light was lit. and the door was unlocked as I, eager but apprehensive, followed Althea into the house. Althea turned on the light and pointing to the left, said, "This is Greg, trapped here in front of his picture window, watching the world go by, waiting for someone who may or may not come home."

Grabbing the wheel chair handles, she wheeled him around toward me, triumphantly chanting, "A well deserved turn about for a philandering, self-centered rat, don't you think?" Not waiting for an answer, she carefully, not tenderly arranged the pillow behind his neck, forcing his head erect.

I had to know, "Is he totally paralyzed? Does he hear you...or us? What can he see with those staring eyes?" I knew I had never seen such strong, but not really definable emotion expressed in someone's eyes before?

"I pray the Bastard can read lips and understand everything he sees," she said while coming over to me and giving me the first kiss, passionate and intense, as if she had not kissed for years. I knew by now, even without seeing it in Greg's anguished eyes, that I was not the first sailor pleasured to torture him! Yet, I too was trapped. Trapped by my needs and aroused by the promises in Althea's smoldering kiss. I would do anything Althea wanted, pretending it was for me, not just to punish Greg.

She wheeled Greg into the next room, fussing over him, leaving him turned to face the bed. I followed compliantly, uninvited but knowing I must, like the lambs meekly following the Judas Ram up the ramp to the killing floor of a slaughter-house. I sat on the bed, where she pointed, facing Greg, while Althea drew the drapes and turned up all the room's lights.

I was wary of what I should do, until Althea dropped to her knees before me. I could see over her head that Greg's staring eyes were taped open! After an illicit hour of torturing Greg, pleasing me, Althea collapsed in sleep. No longer concupiscent, I lay sweaty and spent, unable to sleep, guilt ridden but weary and satiated. Guilt lost, I slept.

Several hours later, I awakened, completely spent, pleasantly aware of how intensely I had been satisfied but ashamed of my role in Althea's revenge. I managed to pull my arm from under Althea's head without waking her. Still exulting that I had performed so well, I felt she was exhausted enough to sleep soundly with the night light still on. I would never know why Greg felt the need to seek his passion elsewhere or what had caused his paralyzing stroke. Asleep, the mad frenzy that had frightened me, no longer demoniacally twisted Althea's face. She was beautiful, her sins now expiated. I tried not to look toward Greg, knowing those eyes would be still sleepless and accusing. Was that hatred for me, Althea or himself?

I Dressed hurriedly in the half lit bedroom, afraid to confront Althea who might demand more of me and too ashamed to look in Greg's wide open eyes, fearing I would see directly into his tormented brain. I knew that I must free the imprisoned Greg, and Althea from this continuing horror show, or forever see Greg's eyes, boring into my soul.

I would never know how many other sailors had willingly inflicted retribution on Greg, but I would be the last. Standing, disheveled but mostly dressed, I dared to look again in his eyes and found softness or a pleading gaze like eyes remembered from a napalmed child, waiting impatiently to die. I reached out with my right hand as if to gently pat His cheek, and then impulsively pinched both nostrils shut, between my thumb and forefinger. With my other hand, I covered his mouth so he could not breathe, yet there was no protest or resistance. The hatred in Greg's eyes was soon gone but I will forever hope it was replaced with gratitude. I quietly opened the door and walked toward what I hoped was my highway, thankful that Althea had not asked me my name, rank or serial number.

BELT A FAT COMEDIAN

Pee Wee Normus, a very big man, was not comfortable flying coach. Once each millennium was enough to re-stoke his memory banks with joke material about the hazards of flying. Now, with two full time script writers, there was no reason for him to suffer for his comedic art. Thirty-five years of mingling with common folk had been a necessity, but now he deserved first class in all accommodations. Pee Wee strained again to close his safety belt, inhaling deep and stretching upward, while pulling with hands beefy but still strong from twice daily cow-milking chores as a young man on the family farm. That farm, small and debt ridden did not have modern equipment. Milking cows made for great hand strength but the safety belt remained and inch short.

"Are you all right, Mister," inquired the solicitous and skinny Grandmother in the window seat. "Should I beep the stewardess? We're going to take off any minute."

"Naw, Lady. My face is always red, and my eyes bulge because my brain's too big," Pee Wee blurted, angry that he, a very successful comedian with a vast repertoire of put-downs could not manage a better mind-your-own-business retort. Cutting down innocent or unwary victims was his specialty.

The busy-body shrunk back in her seat and Maynard Normus felt just a bit guilty, although her concern was an un-invited intrusion into his privacy. Pee Wee's analyst had said he had an inordinate dislike of criticism and even greater fear of ridicule or any form of embarrassment. Not in those words, of course, but in idiomatic and pretentious terms common with his two-hundred dollar an hour billings. In fact, the analyst had said all heavy-set comedians focused on themselves as target of ridicule. implying that Maynard's shtick of skillfully picking on other victims was a bit perverted. It paid off in Cadillacs and Florida Beach condos, and left Pee Wee without guilt, even if his sarcastic humor traveled only one-way. On stage, Pee Wee would only use a hand held microphone, zealously gripped, irrationally afraid someone he targeted would somehow respond to his hilarious and often cruel indictment of their flaws. No one ever dared try to wrest away the microphone dwarfed in his meaty paw.

Pee Wee noticed the older Stewardess with the stern authoritarian look, acquired by twenty years of stewardship quieting panics and suppressing any form of insubordination, was now imperiously nearing, checking each passenger for unfastened belt or reclined seat. Desperate, Pee Wee decided to escape notice burying the unfastened ends in his huge hands, camouflaging his unfastened status. Hands clasped, eyes closed, he seemed a well dressed four hundred pound Buddha lost in self-contemplation and the vigilant Stewardess passed.

Fearful that his seat companion was aware of his subterfuge, and could complain, Pee Wee turned a friendlier face her way and whispered, 'Guys my size don't bounce around much, like a little-bitty sweety like you. I usually buy three tickets, but this time, only two," pointing at the empty middle seat. She stayed silent but managed a brief, weak smile.

Still tired from his heated tirade with the Ticket Agent who didn't extend Maynard the usual upgrade exacerbated by the long and futile run trying to catch the flight made Pee Wee very tired. He closed his eyes to nap. In an instant, he fell into an uncomfortable and sweaty reverie before the ascending plane had retracted its flaps. As flight 737 vectored toward Hubert Humphrey airport in Minneapolis, nine-hundred miles west of La Guardia, Pee Wee revisited another haunting episode from his youth.

Once again he stood, still in his jockstrap, hoping somehow to escape the ignominy of a nude shower with his freshman gym classmates. 'Shag' Bartness, once Iowa Teacher College's Athlete of the Year, but now only a hirsute and paunchy physical education instructor deprived of the somewhat prestigious title of assistant football coach, leered at his blushing pupil.

Not knowing why, Pee Wee hated how thoroughly Shag inspected each boy and provoked demeaning persiflage on the anatomies of his charges. Proud of his over-sized phallus, Shag paraded nude in front of his seventh and eighth grade students somewhat longer than the normal standards of propriety, but not enough to justify indictment or censure from his suspicious but careful Principal.

It was not Shag who first named Maynard, 'Pee Wee', but he sure made it official with his searing falsetto rendition of that scarring sobriquet. Pee Wee probed his daydream's memory bank for the identity of the better endowed classmate, who called him 'Pee Wee', hopeful to effectuate retribution now that he had money and its resultant power. That accursed tag may have been inaugurated byScott Bergen, his old rival for Becky, who chose not to label him Slim or Jester, which were more apt pseudonyms. It was Scott who informed the beautiful Becky Ludwig that Maynard was suffering late puberty, and in front of a dozen giggling classmates, who would join in, forever branding him 'Pee Wee'.

Too bad, Scott didn"t come back from Viet Nam. Pee Wee would've roasted him this weekend when he, who was, the most successful graduate of Lincoln High School"s class of 1965, addressed his classmates at their thirty-fifth reunion party. What delightful ridicule he"d make of Scott's un-stellar accomplishments that led him to seek a career in the army. A lowly buck sergeant, in the ground-pounding infantry, no less.

Pee Wee had always been extra-sensitive. His ability to sense what other people wanted to avoid or hide had granted him empathy for others, and he employed that warmness to win popularity in High School, but his tolerance of other people's peculiarities never seemed reciprocated. Teasing bothered him until he realized, he could disarm any antagonist, by topping their best putdowns with more clever self-directed barbs of his own. When he became seriously overweight, he had more opportunities and much denigrating material. His skill at quick witticisms became known to others. Pee Wee attracted crowds and was reborn, a comedian.

Now successful, he no longer laughed at himself. His earlier sensitivity now was an antenna which still picked up most stranger"s secrets they tried to keep hidden and found unthinkable to face or discuss. When Pee Wee set a target for his humor, he was merciless, and funny to those not targeted.

"Will you have the chicken or roast beef snack?" inquired the prettier of the two coach-class stewardesses, not sure whether to wake the dozing comedian whom she suspected was somebody.

Mention of food, immediately awakened Pee Wee. "I'll have both, ma'am, and if they're any good, you can bring me seconds. When I'm left hungry, I'm mighty dangerous for any pretty gal getting within biting distance. Seriously, I haven't eaten for three days and I'm about to float away. Bring me the sandwich for that skinny guy in the front row, he must be allergic to food."

Not wanting to answer and provoke more wise-cracks, the prudent stewardess who also stretched her uniform but only slightly because of rigid dieting, produced two more sandwiches, then judiciously fled.

Although Pee Wee no longer needed to have all present focus their attention on him, it was unavoidable when he ate. Pee Wee always dined in private because he could not trust his table manners. Rare dinner dates were shocked on first exposure to the spectacle of Pee Wee Normus wolfing down food. When Pee Wee was unhappy, he used food as a palliative but with no more enthusiasm than when he celebrated his good times also with great quantities of food and drink.

Amanda, his intimidated seat companion watched him eat in horror, and lost her appetite. She offered him her sandwich and cupcake, knowing he would not refuse. Now aware of her seat companion's disability, Amanda was no longer intimidated. She tried again her usual familiarity with strangers, "I had a good breakfast with my husband. He woke up early to take me to the airport, although he's retired and pretty crippled with arthritis. A real sweetheart still, after forty five years of marriage."

Mouth full with a sandwich in both hands, Pee Wee refrained from zinging her. Pee Wee had been happily married, three times. First to Becky, almost thirty-five years ago. He had persisted and won the battle for Becky, and married right after graduation. At first, they considered themselves rich. Pee Wee writing copy for KNAK radio, with nights off to do his stand up humor gigs while Becky cashiered at Red Owl. Their first month of marriage was one prolonged honeymoon, in spite of her advancing pregnancy.

"That's real nice lady, and I envy the man enjoying your company for forty-five years. I'm just divorced, again, so I can't make forty-five years of marriage. Reckon I better shoot for marrying forty-five times." Pee Wee liked that line, and the half shocked, half amused look on Amanda's face.

"Are you somebody famous or funny? I mean, is that your job?" she said, obviously incredulous. His face was familiar, and two hundred pounds lighter, Pee Wee had been leading-man handsome. "Should I be asking for your autograph?"

"Well I try to be funny but I ran into one sweet little old lady on an airplane who didn't even know my name. I gave her my autograph in disappearing ink." Pee Wee relaxed his masking grip on the seatbelt fastenings to give Amanda an autographed picture from his coat pocket, then realized he exposed his unhooked belt.

Aghast, Amanda screeched, "Your belt isn't fastened.

"Just shut up lady, I'll fasten up when the captain announces our landing approach," he said so angry that his face burned with embarrassment. In reflexed defense, Pee Wee retreated into the past. He imagined again Becky's pubescent beauty. He had fallen in love with her, almost forty years ago. She was so beautiful and very popular with all the town kids. What chance did he, a gangly and shabbily dressed farm kid, who smelled of the cows he tended each morning, until his father drank away the farm forced his family to town.

He still remembered their first encounter. Pee Wee was at the town beach, the summer, before his frosh year. She was so mature and he physically deserved his nickname. His new swimming suit of black knit wool so delineated his manhood disparagingly that he had rolled up one of his socks, and inserted it in the crotch. Glancing down, examining himself without benefit of mirror, he was impressed. It was so easy to hide one's limitations.

He was flabbergasted that the very popular Becky had allowed him to walk her home. Later, swinging together on her front porch swing, Becky had asked why one of the socks he was wearing was wet. How fiery red he had blushed, implicating himself of some hidden sin that he only imagined she divined. Seeing Pee Wee Normus, brash class cutup and clown impervious to insult or ridicule, turn into a blushing and stammering fool had endeared him to Becky because that proved he was tender and humble. Ah yes, sweet Becky, who stuck with him through those difficult teen years but then grew bitter and vengeful with the birth of their sudden baby, a surprising consequence of his insistence on reward for taking her to the Senior Prom. She never forgave him nor let him forget his guilt, even when he did the right thing by proposing. He never forgave her, when their two year old son, and only child died, even though he knew Becky"s genetics and maternal care were not the cause. Pee Wee faulted his young wife for her supposed resentment toward the baby, harboring evil wishes that came true.

Darrell Dean Normus, Pee Wee's only child would now be thirty-four. Four other wives since Becky had not provided heirs to compete for the money that went to support ex-wives. Pee Wee looked forward to the class reunion and wished that it would allow him to see Becky, again. Many times he dreamed he was back with his first family, but Becky had also died of slow suicide from gin and other memory altering chemicals.

Jeanine, his second wife had been a classmate too, and might be at the reunion. Becky had called her ex-friend, Jeanine, seeking the reason why Pee Wee left her, then reciprocated, giving Jeanine more of Pee Wee's personal baggage than even his therapists collected.

Using Pee Wee's tipsy confession of his rolled sock solution for his inadequacy, Jeanine had formed an embarrassing interpretation of the wet sock vignette in her public denigrations of Pee Wee, topping him at his own game. Her version expressed her preference for the wet sock instead of the real article. Those amusing assaults on her husband's ego shortened Pee Wee's second marriage to weeks. She would surely be at the reunion exhibiting her third husband, who was even younger than the last.

Pee Wee awakened from his discomfiting dream to find the nastier stewardess shaking his shoulder, loudly remonstrating. "We have begun our approach to Minneapolis. Fasten your seatbelt or I will call the Captain. Hurry before we lose our landing slot."

Pee Wee sucked in deep, face purpling as he held his breath and tugged with all of his strength on his disconnected seatbelts as if they might benevolently stretch. His vision of the confronting stewardess dimmed as he pulled harder on the nearly connected belts. With a last desperate tug, intense pain in his massive left arm did convulsively force the clasping of the breath stifling safety belt. Explosively, Pee Wee's lungs emptied of their retained air, but none returned. His strained heart muscles begged for oxygen, without success. The World would not laugh at Pee Wee again, and nobody would be humiliated at his class reunion.

EATING WISE
A health food addict named Spratt
would nag his plump wife to tears
for healthy Jack would never eat fat
yet she was widowed twenty years.

BLACK AND WHITE

I was reminded of the comedian, Redd Foxx the minute he entered Carla's Classic Coffee Shop. Scruffy and wearing a suit Salvation Army would reject, he was in stark contrast to his elegantly garbed, tall blonde male companion. Yet, they were closely, almost intimately linked together, although their contrasting mien and manner begged for explanation. Obviously, they came from different worlds but were now linked together by a strange mutuality or quirk of fate. Despite their odd pairing, they seemed physically closer than normal as they clumsily walked, crab-like through the crowded room, almost arm in arm, to the first open table. Then, I discovered their common bond.

The sloppy colored fellow with the bad complexion had his right hand-cuffed to the taller white man's left hand who graciously masked their necessary link using the charitable placement of his newspaper. They drew my attention away from the excellent swiss-steak, deliciously smothered in rich mushroom and onion gravy. Carla's Wednesday special was better than usual with a real-life exhibition for my speculation and entertainment.

I was lunching alone and had time to kill before my two o'clock appointment, upstairs with Doctors Monroe and Simmons. There I would introduce our new generic match of 'Blocto IV'. Had I worked wiser, scheduling ahead, I would have been dining sumptuously at the River Bluffs Country Club, charming the good doctors with my anecdotes and my more than adequate and much appreciated expense account.

I disliked waiting in Peoria's busiest medical clinic, stuffed with gabby parents and crying children, so I stalled, eating slowly and closely observing the eating habits of the wide variety of Carla's lunch customer's. Much more interesting than upstairs with the usually
irritated patients suffering their time distorting and endless wait for dispensation of medical miracle. Sadly, the Clinic's staff was

handicapped by more patients than available time and only mortal. I was happier waiting at Carla's where a diverse procession of healthy and hungry people allowed me my favored habit of studying people.

Over the years of detailing pharmaceuticals, I have acquired accurate insights into people's character and condition. If a man looks like a bum and smells like a bum, that's what he probably is. One can observe and guess about the background of people passing by, but we seldom get the opportunity to check our perceptions, or the accuracy of our assumptions.

The disheveled captive and his elegant captor, were appealing targets for serious speculation. Possibly material for an interesting anecdote I would beneficially use to amuse my clientele, if I could divine just what crime was done and the eventual punishment. I could only guess at the background on the perpetrator, but that was the downside of people watching. You don't have any way to check the accuracy of your speculations.

The short sullen dark man was concentrating on holding the menu in his left hand, doing all the listening, probably somewhat penitently. From where I was sitting, I could not overhear their conversation, but from their lip movements, the shorter miscreant with beard stubble and oversized teeth seemed to be slurring his words. I hate hearing speakers drop syllables from words that should not be contracted. The poor miscreant was mumbling stiff-lipped and poorly enunciated speech and even without hearing, I could discern his poor language skills just watching his mouth. You see, I practice my articulation before a mirror and find oral motility interesting and quite revealing.

The short and sloppy criminal's stiff-lipped smile could be an effort to mask poor dental work such as provided criminals at most penal institutions. That weak smile occurred but once during the time I watched their conversation. His bleak future probably gave him nothing to smirk about.

The sophisticated, taller gentleman seemed much too prosperous and polished to be just a common cop, more likely to be an officer of the law more lavishly rewarded than common policemen. He had to be an able communicator, a mutual skill I practice before mirrors and easily identify in others from the facial mannerisms and their calculated word pauses. He seemed out of place with the coarse criminal, his captive certainly had to be.

The fast moving, freckled waitress with her pert smile and dimpled cheeks dropped off their menus and water and did not seem concerned that her diners were bunched together, not normally placed, and could be assumed to be holding hands. Either she was not a strong student of people like myself, or she was used to a wide diversity of customers, unaware of their peculiarities. When she had served me, I had mused on the reason for the small bird tattooed on her forearm and now wondered if her milieu was similar to the captured prisoner. Birds obviously signified freedom or escape. Distracted, my eyes followed her hip-swaying gait as she paraded toward the kitchen.

Later, while the fascinating duo consumed Carla's always featuring and economically nourishing but blander meat loaf special, I focused on the pairs" differing table manners. The Foxx look alike had his right hand clomped around his fork in the manner of a child first using table ware, shoveling food toward his mouth, which he neglected to keep politely closed while chewing. I could see food juices to dribbling unattended down his chin unshaved chin.

In stark contrast, his loftier master, also restricted to using but one hand, elegantly transporting food deftly into his mouth, neatly ingesting even the gravy without requiring mop ups with his napkin. I was again distracted from my scrutiny of the odd couple when the cute waitress asked me if I wished a serving of Carla's famous pie. Determining that it came with the special, I decided on mince. Although quite full, I still had twenty minutes to kill, so I asked for ice cream and coffee too. I did wonder why the

-28-

distinguished member of the mystery pair knew about and frequented Carla's as he too, seemed a trifle out of place. Excusable lapse of taste, if one knew that the food quality made up for the shoddier working class ambiance.

When my attention again turned to the linked pair, they were clumsily standing. The tall, enigmatic gentleman was risking exposition of their linked status by compassionately allowing his prisoner bathroom privileges. A grant that the miscreant was not expecting or habituated to, for he stood clumsily, hampered by handcuffs.

As he attempted to straighten his poorly draped and cheaply tailored sport jacket, I got a fleeting glance of the small revolver holstered to hide in the small of his back! I knew I must warn his seemingly unaware keeper of the hidden gun before his prisoner made a break for freedom. As they both clumsily walked toward the back corner of the dining room where a small sign indicated restrooms, I decided to risk involvement, afraid that their trip to the toilet might provide the criminal an unfortunate opportunity to escape.

They were awkwardly standing at the urinals, and I seized the opportunity, standing to the right of the patient and waiting lawman. I cleared my throat, getting his attention. Then I said, very softly but distinctly, "Your prisoner has a gun hidden in the small of his back!"

He looked at me strangely, not grateful, but amused. He said, "Yes, I know he's got a gun, if he didn't, I'd be long gone. Fact is, if I had the gun he'd be one embarrassed black cop and I'd be gone like spit on a hot griddle.

The Redd Foxx look alike, who apparently was the real gun-bearing cop laughed and laughed, and I sadly realized this was one anecdote I should never share with my customers.

BURN!

With exaggerated theatrics for the benefit of his menacing antagonist, Greg flipped open his mobile phones as if he were calling 911, but pushed the auto re-dial of his sweetheart's number, and crooned, "Hey Babe, how ya doing?"

Greg's four-year-old Volkswagen had but one luxury and that was the road safe hands-free speaker phone, which he would normally use, when not emulating a highway patrol safety-snitch. Beth answered before the second ring. "Calling so soon? You must have really hated to leave!"

"Don't flatter yourself, Beth. I am calling only because I want the ten-wheeler that's riding my bumper to think I am calling the law."

"Give him his passing lane, Darling? You never drive over the limit. Obeying California's speed laws can make people angry and dangerous on the freeways!"

"I am already going five miles over the limit, and in the left to pass a cautious old coot driving a beautiful old Studebaker Lark, and I am looking it over."

"You have got your nerve calling anyone a cautious old coot. We've been engaged almost two years. That's cautious!"

Greg smothered a guilty snicker, and switched the subject away from the second delay of their wedding. "I guess the trucker's not an old car buff. He's up on my bumper, and flashing lights. Guess he thinks I'm in his private passing lane."

"Honey, switch on your headlights, He will think it's the stoplight and back-off" He did, and the massive truck radiator seemed to fill his back seat.

"That was a bad idea, sweetheart. Now the damned fool is really mad. He's right on my butt!"

Beth felt the hairs on her neck stiffen and shouted, "Skip principals, pull over to the left."

"I did, and he followed me over. He must be having a very bad day."

"Did you try speeding up?" Beth said, knowing that Greg had never drove recklessly or sped, even when late or impatient.

"Honey, I'm going seventy-five and I don't think my little bug can go faster. He must be empty cause he stayed with me. I'm going to really nudge the brakes."

"Shee-it! He actually bumped my bumper. I want to get away from this maniac"

"What kind of nut are you dealing with?"

"Beth, he's dangerous! He's a semi pulling a tanker. They should be extra cautious."

"That's dangerous cargo, Baby, lose him, and turn off on the next exit."

"I did, and he followed me. Must be a psycho. Write down this number. I think it is AAK 229 omething. Maybe 3 or 8. I"m going to really call 911."

"No, I will. You concentrate on driving with both hands, or switch to the hands-off phone. Where are you?"

"I turned off 405 at Ridge Road. I will make the call, and explain better. Love you. Bye"

Beth didn"t hear about the accident for almost two hours on the six-thirty news. A one car accident on Ridge Road, driver's name not released, yet. Beth knew. She called the police and told them how a gas hauler harassed her sweetheart about that area, and the dispatcher impassively said, "Fill out a report. We will see if there was a trucker involved, but we cannot release identities of drivers by their license number, and all your evidence is tainted, or second-hand.

Weeks passed and Beth's anguish increased instead of fading as her friends had prayed would happen. Beth carefully wrapped her engagement ring in tissue and hid it deep in the futilely filled cedar hope-chest along with her first RN pin from Saint Timothy'sNursing School along with her accumulated Girl

Scout pins and Saint Benadicts High School awards, and moved on with her life. The overwhelming desire for revenge came that first night sleeping alone, but grief management sessions and consoling sessions with her childhood minister, who had promised to marry Beth and Greg as his last pastoral duty before retirement..

Formally resigned, Pastor Bunnery vainly tried to help Beth suppress her desire for vengeance. Beth told all her concerned friends that her obsession to find the oppressive truck was not just vengeance motivated. That anonymous driver was a continuing menace, and she was dedicated to get him off the road before he anymore malicious deaths separated loved ones,

Two years passed quickly. Too quickly to allow the Highway Patrol to do anything about Greg's crash, or discovery of the accident facts. Beth seemed to be adjusting to her loss, except for the disconcerting habit of talking to her Teddy Bear, and in fact, receiving responses, that only she heard. The toy bear was the only remnant of her romance with Greg. He had chosen the tawny bear with shortly frizzled fur because it matched her hairstyle, and chose the bear to carry her engagement ring and marriage proposal in its tiny briefcase.

Beth did not have duty at Saint Timothy's Hospital, until Midnight and she and Bear customarily used all their free-time provocatively cruising her convertible back on forth on Interstate 405, looking. Beth said, "This will be the last run, Bear. I need a quick nap before work."

Bear said, "You say that every night and we still keep trolling roads for Greg's killer! Everyone tells you to leave it to the law. Not me! Let's do the run again. You said that truckers usually run repeat routes and we have been ready for a long time."

Beth gave Bear a reassuring hug, then U-turned her top-down convertible down the entrance and drove north just over the limit in the passing lane, ignoring one finger salutes, flashing lights and impatient horns. Each time, she smiled brightly and waved friendly-like when they passed to her right, but none truck passed without getting Beth and her bear's close scrutiny of their license plate.

Traffic was heavy and she appraised four ten-wheelers in the next fifteen miles before the Red Freightliner pulling a tanker sounded its strident horn. Beth new immediately it was the one. The last license digit was 'B', not 3 or 8. She slowed and the trucker took the bait. Up on her bumper, less than three feet separated them. She turned on her headlights. The impatient trucker hit his airbrakes as her tail light glowed red, then resumed even closer pursuit. She repeated the irksome baiting twice, each time, the tanker decreased the distance between them. The next exit was not Ridge road, but Beth thought the angered semi-driver was ready. Beth swung left onto Slope Road, and the Freightliner followed, tires squealing on the tight turn up the exit.

A mile down the road, Beth swung to the center of the narrow roadway and slowed. In her mirror, the giant truck seemed already in the back seat of her small Le Baron. Beth secured the steering wheel with upraised knees, then turned and fired the widow maker at the radiator, twice. The steel-jacketed slug tore through the radiator like berries through a bird. Onward, the slug tore, shattering the camshaft gear. Out of time valves smashed into the pistons, bending rods and fracturing the crankshaft. The engine changed from a roaring dynamo turning three thousand revolutions a minute into a solid mass. The rear driven wheels locked, and the trailer jack-knifed, wrapping around the cab, and swinging the rig into screeching rollover, turning the cab upside down, crushing the cab down, immobilizing both cabin doors.

Beth sped off beyond sight before stopping to remove the dummy license plate, then u-turned and drove back. "We can safely blend in with the rubber-neckers, Bear" as she cradled her precious bear in her arms to see the fiery denouement of her lover's assassin.

Cars had already stopped and a gathering crowd peered through the crumpled windows of the overturned semi cab. The driver limply hung limply upside down suspended by his safety belt. The stench of the diesel fuel seemed over powering, but reminded Beth of the unused zippo lighter she carried in her jacket, to remind her of her victory over her tobacco addiction, when Greg had first challenged her to quit. Greg gone, she couldn't resume the habit Greg thought repulsive.

The curious crowd might be endangered, but in their midst, she could easily flick and drop the lighter with no one wiser. Diesel fuel would not explode so everyone would pull back, and none of them would know the source of the incinerating flames. At that moment, she saw the windshield reddening from arterial blood spewing unhindered from the driver, who was now imploring the onlookers for help. His lips were silently mouthing, "Help me!"

Beth dropped the un-opened Zippo and instinctively dove down to the drivers door. "Back away and stop anyone from smoking," Beth shouted. She tugged at the crumpled door, securely wedged then flailed away the imprisoning glass shards, without regard for cuts or fingers.

She was small and supple enough to squeeze in and squat on the roof, directly confronting the despised driver. Their eyes were inches apart, and she could smell second-hand beer, even over the spilled fuel. A gash usually below but now above his eyes, exposed the bloody sinus cavity, where blood welled and flowed copiously, but that was not the source. Beth searched, then found an ugly gash on his right forearm just above hand that still gripped the useless steering wheel. Beth had no problem finding the good pressure point on the inner arm and the blood no longer painted the crumpled windshield.

"I'm going to die, aren't I," whimpered the driver and Beth resisted telling him that had been her ardent wish. His head was swollen from striking the massive large steering wheel or the shattered windshield, probably with a life threatening fracture. Both legs dangled back down, broken, but barely bleeding.

"You will live!" Beth said, wondering why she wasted so

much time seeking this man's death.. Life saving must become addictive, for those who do it, she concluded.

BURYING GRANDPA

Le Center's schools closed for summer vacation almost a week ago and nothing exciting had happened yet. My new Buck Rogers rocket watch said it was nine o'clock, and my cousin Billy was still slopping down breakfast. I made tons of noise while waiting outside on the back stoop hoping that would speed him up. Already too late to go fishing, but we would probably try anyway. We hadn't caught anything but bullheads, so far, and they were the only fish I couldn't eat, if I had both caught and or cleaned the ugly mud suckers. Billy would and did, though. He would eat anything yet he was as skinny as I and almost as tall. Except for Eunice and Merle, I was the tallest kid in sixth grade at Central Elementary.

"Billy! That's enough cornflakes. You've had two bowls already, and your Dad will want something to puke out, if he ever gets up. Put your bowl in the sink, and go try waking wake your Dad," Aunt Mary shouted. I stopped whistling and whittling with my new scout knife, and hunkered down quiet.

'Dang!' Billy's Dad had been on a toot, again. Usually, he just fell of the wagon on Saturday nights, but this was Saturday and a half workday for Uncle Boog, at the Le Center Creamery where he was the newly promoted Chief Cheese-maker and apprentice drunk. Friday drunks were dangerous.

Our Grandpa Kelly was an Irish bartender and that made him an expert on boozing. Grandpa always said that no one was a drunkard unless they got drunk two days in a row. I hoped Uncle Boog wouldn't qualify, drunk again on Saturday.

It seemed hours and still no Billy, but time passed slow waiting while our short and precious summer vacation zoomed away. At last, the screen door banged open, and Billy came out quietly, followed by his quite healthy and surprisingly alert father. Boog Kelly, who should have been at the creamery. "Well, now who's this starved bum sitting on my steps, waiting for a handout. Damned if he don't look like me brother's child, Gary." He tousled my hair with affection and said, "My nephew, Gary wouldn't sit on the back stoop, like he wasn't welcome at our table."

Billy winked, and started unlocking his bicycle tethered to the porch railing, as if somebody would steal that rickety hand- me-down bicycle. "Hello, Uncle Boog," I said, hoping for a quick and uncomplicated get-a-way.

"Tell your Mom, not to buy any cheese dated, June 6, 1951, as it won't be Le Center's finest. I took the day off to mourn and bury me Dad and my helper, ain't quite got the hang of cheesemaking yet." It was then, I noticed the large stoneware crock he was holding. Grandpa had died last fall, racing the Great Northern Streamliner to the Lexington road crossing, turning Grandpa and his rickety old pickup into bug splatter. Because the collision caused Grandpa's fresh brew of homemade Irish whiskey to explode, cremation was the family's logical choice for his remains. Unfortunate because most Le Center Lutherans believe that you arise from the grave on Judgement Day, just as you are instead of how you was.

I was curious why Uncle Boog waited until today, to bury his Dad"s ashes and why he chose a Friday for a night of mourning, instead of Saturday, when he could sleep late. I was curious enough to ask, "Where you going to put Grandpa?" not at all sure that I wanted to know, or that Uncle Boog would tell me the real truth. He always teased, like Grandpa did when officiating in his saloon, always filled, including even non alcoholics folks there just to hear his wild stories. Those listeners usually drank Kelly's home made genuine Sarsparilla and Nerve Tonic, thinking that it was alcohol free.

That locally famous drink provide Billy's and my main source of income, until Dad started teaching me the value of a dollar by working, for him at Gunder's Cosmetics mail order house. You see, Grandpa bought all the bottles for his elixir from

Billy and me. We gathered all sorts of empty bottles, getting two cents for beer bottles and a penny for ketchup or pop bottles. Grandpa bottled his elixir only in bottles Billy and I supplied. We had an exclusive, locked-in market.

Grandpa brewed his locally famous nerve tonic in a large cauldron just like witches use. Some folks said, it was mostly alcohol, catnip and wild hemp, but Grandpa never let anyone watch him mix his drink, so they could only guess.

Uncle Boog, took a long time to answer like he was just deciding, "Grandpa, always wanted to travel, and never did. He loved to visit with people, really get inside them and see what they believe. I think I will go to the creamery, grind up his ashes with the peppercorns for our pepper cheese, and let him travel everywhere we send our cheese." Uncle Boog, thinking on that picture, paled and set down the crock on the top step and holding both hands over his mouth to keep from up-chucking last night's goodies, and scooted back in the house.

"He was teasing, wasn't he?" I asked Billy, remembering how Uncle Boog fooled you except when you thought he was, he wasn't. "Remember how he threatened to tan your butt for selling Grandpa, that case of empty beer bottles, and we thought he was teasing?"

Billy rubbed his butt, while remembering that walloping, and said, "He was sorry later. Just the thought of all that beer going to waste made him loony, and he blamed me."

Billy and I had found a case of beer hidden in a culvert under the tracks by the lake we fish. It meant nothing to us, except as empty bottles worth two cents, and we had uncapped and emptied the whole case, taking the empties to Grandpa's 'Sit-a-Bit' Tavern.

Boog had seen Billy returning the borrowed bottle opener to the kitchen drawer, and insisted on knowing why it was borrowed. Billy was not a good liar like me, though I sure have coached him.

Grandpa had thought Boog's outrage was funny, and told everyone but Uncle Boog didn't laugh, even politely,
but his face stayed red a long time.

"We can't let him do it," I said. "Maybe that would poison people, or make their teeth fall out like Grandpas." Billy nodded agreement, Shushing me, and grabbing hold of the crock. We carried it back to the woodshed and garage, at the end of the lot, then returned and started a game of mumble-dy-peg with my new knife, while we waited for Uncle Boog to reappear. I had Billy forced to pull the almost buried peg with his teeth when we heard the telephone ring demandingly, and soon Uncle Boog came out, almost running.

"Tell Ma, I"m at the creamery, my assistant walked off the job." He loped down the alley toward the creamery on B street, totally forgetting the crocked remains of Grandpa.

My Dad, Boog's brother, was teaching me responsibility, working Saturday afternoons at Gunder's. I swept the floors while everyone was off, and the plant empty. I hated working when others weren't but my Dad wasn't like his brother Boog at all. Dad wanted me to grow a work ethic and learn the real value of money. I had only a couple of fun hours ahead, before my janitorial chores, but I had a grand inspiration. Work wasn't too bad if you had company.

"Hey Billy, I know where to put Grandpa, and he will absolutely love it. Grandpa will travel all over the world and will have intimate contact with lots of beautiful girls. He will love it." I had deliberately used 'intimate', one of Billy's favorite words, since we had looked it up in the school library's big Webster Dictionary. We got confused when the same word meant cuddly and to insinuate.

"Oh, and where's that, pinhead?" he said, casually but I knew I would have him helping me sweep floors in the dusty mixing room, just as surely as Tom Sawyer got had help painting his Aunt's fences.

"At my job!" I answered smugly. "There's a big tank they keep the talcum powder in. We can drop Grandpa's ashes in and the vibrator will mix him in with all the other stuff they blend in the face and body powders. Gunder's ships that stuff all over the world. Gramps would love being slathered on a lot of pretty girl's butts. He never could get close enough to those huge, old ladies that hung out at his tavern."

Not even asking about the work we would have to do first, Billy agreed. We scrounged around in the wood shed for something to put grandpa's ashes in. We needed a handled container so we could carry him on our bikes. We found an empty pail that once held three gallons of pickle pimento's, flavoring for LeCenter's finest pepper cheese but now gathering dust under Grandpa's old workbench. Without spilling any of Grandpa in that dirty old shed, we got him in with the residue of a million dried pimentos. Someone sneezed and I really thought it was Grandpa, until I saw Billy backhand the snotty remains on his jeans.

Gunder's was closed Saturday afternoons but us important personnel without a key, knew a spare hung on a nail under the loading dock. I opened the door and said, "Lets do sweep-up first, and include Grandpa when we dump the sweepings in the mixer."

Billy, just laughed and said, "I knew there was a reason you didn't want to sprinkle Grandpa out the pail while we rode downtown!" I forgot to tell you, that was his brilliant plan. Sprinkling Grandpa all over town, like the water they used to settle the dust on Le Center's streets during summer would be an insult to a man never ever found laying in a gutter, like his youngest son Boog often occupied.

"Okay, we'll mix Grandpa in the powder, first. This week they're making Heavenly Scent. You go fishing alone while I do the sweeping." I grabbed the pail from Billy and walked to the ladder to the steep steps that went to the platform surrounding the top of the powder vat, while Billy debated bugging out. "You can come up, Billy, but don't make any sparks. No smoking because this fine dust is explosive like gunpowder. That's why my job is do important."

Billy mumbled something I didn't catch. He didn't smoke but he always had candy cigarettes he'd selfishly suck on, without sharing. I think cigarette companies made them so kids would think it was cool pretending to smoke. Ma wouldn't let me have them, so I didn't get any when they closed Grandpa's place. Boog and Billy got most of the goodies.

We climbed the scary open grating steps to the top of the mixing bin's platform. It was grating like the steps and you could see the floor, sixteen feet below. The open floor let the slippery powder fall through, instead of piling up, although the iron grill platform was every bit as slick. A noisy belt conveyer delivered big sacks of finely ground flour, stinky flower parts and powdered rock. A neat vibrator and air pump was used to mix the ngredients and fluff it up. I turned it on so Grandpa would be spread thoroughly through the gigantic vat, and soon the level of fluffy powder rose near to the top, though it had been less than half full.

"Pry off the lid, Billy. Be careful of the face powder, it's really slippery stuff and look how far down it is." Billy looked down and reeled with feigned dizziness, then handed me the un-opened pail, and started back down the steps.

I stood, looking at the powder fluffing, prying off the balky lid and slipped when it popped off. Taking three faltering baby steps, to regain balance, one foot plunged over the edge and I slid right under the safety railing, grandpa's pail handle firmly held in my left hand.

I did not float in the fluffed up powder, but grandpa and his pail did, a full arm's length over my head at the powder's surface. The vat full of suffocating powder was much deeper than I could survive, and I wasted many suffocating seconds of frustrated kicking before I realized, what held my right arm erect. Grabbing the pail handle with both hands and chinning myself, I reached the surface and by wrapping my arms around the buoyant pail, get my head high enough to breath.

"Billy, shut off the vibrator," I yelled but my voice was stifled by a mouthful of Heavenly Scent". My vision was blocked by a pasty coating of the talcum. I yelled again, a little louder but Billy did not answer.

Just a little calmer, I realized the seriousness of my predicament, and thought of how I might survive. Firmly holding the can of Grandpa"s ashes, I tried kicking to the side of the bin, but swimming did not work in the fluffed up powder. Blinking did not clear my eyes, so my fate was in the hand of rescuers that would come only if they knew I was there.

"Billy, please get help. You won't be in trouble. I will get the tanning. Please get help," I said in my Sunday company voice. He did not answer. I hoped that he had gone for help, but knew that was a long shot. Billy would not want any part of my predicament because his Dad turned extra mean when he was sick. He was usually just sick Sundays. This week, Uncle Boog had a head start.

The can holding me up was sinking, the fine powder letting out the buoyant air in the bucket, maybe. My dilemma was getting worse and then the Gander's fire alarm began warbling. If the flames reached the powder vat, I would escape, but in a ball of flame, streaking across the town like a Fourth of July sky rocket. I heard the siren of LeCenter's big American-La France fire truck and it came closer. I sniffed for tell tale smoke but could only smell the lilac smell of the sweet smelling junk clogging my nostrils. The siren grew louder.

I heard Gunder's front door burst open and Le Center's volunteer firemen burst into the mixing room, and up the steps. Uncle Boog in his yellow slicker and big fire hat looked big as Superman to me, and mad! "Gregory! Where in Hell did you put Grandpa?" Uncle Boog screamed.

"Mixed in the Heavenly Scent bath powder," I said, worrying whether he would wallop me for losing his Daddy's ashes, or just Billy who must have called the fire department. Then he smiled big, and I could breath.

"You and Billy come by the fire station. Soon as I get out of my gear, we'll go to Whelan's Drug Store and I will buy the three of us a double size chocolate sundae. We've got to do something real important so we will always remember the day we buried grandpa."

We all still do, but for a bunch of different reasons. Boog never did become a professional drinker, but that year his pepper cheese took the blue ribbon at the Minnesota State Fair, even without Grandpa's ashes.

KISSING FROGS
If some frog asks you for a kiss,
implying he'll become a prince,
It is sham, they're not mutated.
If counting on a life of bliss,
accept again my warning hints,
frogs stay frogs when osculated!

CHARLENE, RODEO QUEEN

Charlene regretted her eff-me look that men found so desirable because it always ended with so much sadness. No one believed her to be not yet "sweet-sixteen." She had seen too much of an ugly world, and experience had marred her piquant beauty with a worldliness that did not match her freckled,childlike face.

Now that the body of her last mattress mate had been rudely dropped off in a roadside culvert, Charlene hoped she and her pimp and lover were headed for the Montana mesa where wild horses were free for the taking. She begged, "Aren't we going to get our horses now, Lester?"

Petty snorted, "With only two hundred bucks? We are going back to the casinos. We'll roll another gambler but this time we'll pick one that's won some big dough. Then we'll have enough money to buy a customized trailer and slick saddle for your horse, Just one more trick for my sweet Charlene, and we'll get our wild mustangs, wild and mean."

Without his fumbling guitar accompaniment, their theme song just didn't sound real. Charlene supposed Petty had no intention of getting horses, just money. No sense arguing the point since Petty always won and she was still a baby about pain. "Okay, but turn off the road, I gotta pee." Charlene casually patted her back pocket surreptitiously, and found the bulge from the ice pick she had removed from last night"s poor, dead salesman. Lester didn't know she had removed the pick and kept it. Pulling it out of the victim's back did not bring him back to life, but it made her feel less guilty. She still had the handle wrapped with a handkerchief, hoping that would preserve Charlie's fingerprint, not hers.

Everyone assumed she was dumb. Yet, she had the perfect plan to fool even a schemer like Lester. As she passed the rear of the pickup, she stabbed the sidewall of the tire with the ice pick, held carefully, the bloody handkerchief covering the handle. She heard immediate hissing, and began to loudly sing, "Just one more trick, Charlene..." as she climbed in the passenger seat. Disarmed by her cooperation, Lester started the truck, and shifted into low. Five feet forward, the deflated tire wallowed uselessly while the still inflated driver side tire spun and tossed sand, digging in for the night.

"I musta drove over some cactus and have a goddamned flat. Get your ass here and help me change the tire, Charlene." "Lester, be nice. Just tell me what to do, politely," she said, hopefully, but Lester was engrossed in setting up the bumper jack. He was whistling another of his stupid songs, off-key and disjointed. How could she have ever believed that he was a genuine musician, she wondered, while intently considering the precarious positioning of the flimsy bumper jack. It seemed identical to the one her Mother's live-in boyfriend used when a providential flat tire spared her from the usual back seat chores exacted whenever her Mother worked late. First time, it had been an invitation to go out for a pizza. Maybe running away with Petty had been to escape her Mother's salacious boyfriends, and not her mother, who was nice except when too drunk to satisfy her friends. Charlene did not like to be her sexual surrogate.

Petty restored reality hollering, "Just hold the friggen flashlight so I can change the tire. I'm going to crawl under the back to let down the spare. Don't stand by that screwed-up wimpy jack. Don't even touch the truck. Back off over there and shine that damned light under the truck bed."

Impatient, as always, Lester was slithering under the rear of the truck, and for the first time, she defied his commands, resting her hand lightly on the top of the fully extended jack. "Is this where you need the light, Lester?" and as she spoke she leaned low, using the jack for support. Already unstable and angled outward, it toppled, and the rear of the low rider collapsed downward, pinning Petty under the spare tire carrier.

"Oh shit, Charlene," Petty moaned in a hoarse whisper. "It's got me. Oooh....So...hard...to breathe. Charlene, Sugar. Please help. Dig out sand from under Ugh. Umph....uh my back. Oooh, You can, Please. Use...your hands!" Each time he exhaled, the truck sank lower on his chest.

His lungs emptied but no air returned. Charlene stood where he had first positioned her, but turned off the big flashlight. It was bad enough, listening to Lester trying to kick free, but she could not watch. He could no longer manage words but his fading moans were eloquent testimonial of his losing battle to escape death.

Only when he was silent, did she move toward her partner and once fascinating lover. She cradled her head on his motionless thighs and moaned the song Lester had created for her. It was an appropriate lullaby and dirge.

Deputy Sheriff Grimes, tired from a long boring shift, regretted spotting a crises right at shift's end. Passing by, he could see someone sitting behind the gaudy purple low rider pickup that was pulled discreetly off highway 93 behind the dusty mesquite bushes he had used as cover to poach for speeders. He would be late for his planned evening of chasing girls on the strip, but duty called. He slowed and made a tire-screeching u-turn, and pulled up behind the stolen pickup.

In his headlights, a young girl lay sheltering someone or something, then lifted up her head and stared his way while keaning in a soft mumbling wail, "Just one more trick for the rodeo queen. Then off to our wild mustangs, sweet Charlene."

The California plate matched the alert on his dashboard clipboard. It was stolen. Grimes called in his location, un-holstered his gun and hollered, "Put both your hands in the air, lady and stand facing away from me." Then more loudly, "1, 2, 3, 4,5...." Grimes realized that he could count to one hundred with no response, as she ignored his pointed gun, and sunk lower against a cushioning clump. Grimes could see she was small and very young, and didn't wish to justify shooting a child, righteous or not. He turned to the recording camera and mouthed, "She's not armed or dangerous and seems injured or incapacitated."

Grimes exited the patrol car and moved forward and nudged the recumbent girl with the toe of his shiny black chukka boot. "What the hell, happened here?"

Finally, she looked at him with young but battle hardened eyes that had seen too much of the seamy side of life. He just glared, waiting for her to fill the silence. He won. "My name is Charlene. I was kidnaped, sort of. My boy friend is dead. His name was Lester Petty."

Shining his powerful flashlight in her eyes, he demanded, "Well the registered owner isn't Lester Petty. The truck belongs to Alfred Booker. Did you and your boyfriend steal the truck?"

"I don't think that was the name of the guy who had the truck. Lester sold me to this salesman named Smith for the night, and we all rode in his truck to his motel. Lester twisted my arm until I agreed. Here, see the bruises. That was the first time I ever crossed, Lester and he threatened to kill me if I ever did again. We went to Mr. Smith's room at the Starshine Motel, and Lester said he would wait for me in the bar. It was was really nice. The room, I mean. I spent most of the night, watching that big television. Did you know they show dirty movies right on television. Isn't that against the law in Reno?"

Still holding the accusing light in her eyes, he wondered was she a victim or victor. Lester had to be guilty of statutory rape, as Charlene could not be more than fifteen, although the kidnaping would seemed problematical, at best. "I promised to let Lester into the room after the guy was asleep. He didn't take very long at all before he was asleep. I thought he was kind of nice. I never would've killed him. Lester took the truck keys out of Mr. Smith's pants pocket."

Developing belief, Deputy Grimes doused the inquisitive light, avoiding the hurt look of a trapped and tortured animal that lurked in her eyes. "So how did Lester kill Smith? Did you help Lester in any way?"

"No, it was all Lester's doing. He took the money and the keys. Even the money Smith promised me."

"Did you and Petty plan to rob Smith and take his truck right from the the start?"

"No, we were thumbing and walking. The Smith guy didn't have much money but Lester said he reminded him of his parole officer. Lester left him under a bridge a few miles back toward Sparks. I begged Lester to let him go but he stabbed him with this ice pick. Stabbed him in the back just once. I guess he knew where. I saved the ice pick with Lester's fingerprints on it, for the police."

"Stand still right in that spot, Charlene, and toss me the icepick, handle first." Deputy Grimes picked up the murder weapon in with a kleenex, and secured it in the trunk, under his control. Then he swung his patrol car around, facing the highway and away from the stolen pickup, his dash mounted camera now focused on the highway and the access driveway. He would justify this action as protecting the scene by focusing on potential intruders and being visible to the oncoming accident investigation team. Only two years on the force, and he was already part of a murder investigation. Too bad, he couldn't have figured in the capture of the perpetrator.

He motioned the girl and she came, obediently. "You can wait here in air conditioned comfort in the back seat. Don't try the doors, Charlene. They lock automatically. I need to go back and check one more thing." This far out from Reno, Grimes would have at least one hour to get acquainted with fascinating Charlene before the investigators would arrive, but he would be more careful this time, not desiring another ugly session with internal affairs.

Grimes looked down at Petty. Grimes was experienced enough to know the investigators would find that Petty had suffered, the weight of the collapsed pickup on his chest which had impaired his breathing, and oxygen starved blood, had painted his lips blue, as proof. Petty had not been crushed, but slowly suffocated, probably begging Charlene to re-jack the truck. Grimes took out his western bandanna and wiped the handle and rack of the lowered jack, pacing particular attention to the release latch on the ratchet. It was now an accident, to even the most suspicious investigators.

Whistling approximately the catchy melody of Charlene's song, Deputy Grimes returned to his patrol car, opened the back door, and beckoned Charlene to come out. He had sprawled a rumpled blanket out near the rear of the patrol car. Charlene too, had Lester's song on her mind, and realized, just one more trick for the rodeo queen. She had not escaped but did have a new manager and probably needed a new icepick.

A FEAST

George Washington Jones sat down at the small table, with little desire to eat, but determined to consume every crumb of the feast spread before him. The ostentatious setting on starched linen, promised the finest meal he would ever eat. All of his favorite foods awaited under the salver's covers plus a few elegant delicacies Jones saw only in old movies, Though he was eating alone, George had an audience so he would not disappoint the staff, although he was imposter, and this splendid feast was meant for someone else.

No matter. By the time the State found out that he did not deserve the almost royal service or selection of all food choices, George would be long gone. He would not leave an assessable estate, and for all he cared, they could exhume him from the prison's burial plot, and sell his bones to a fertilizer plant. Jones, number 847653, had warned his keepers, they were executing an innocent man.

CHRISTMAS AT DEER LODGE

Wisps of powder snow filtered through the imperfectly sealed front window to form a scarlet haze surrounding the 'WELCOME TO CHIEF'S BAR' sign. It was Christmas eve and I was the only customer brought in by the sign's coaxing.

The streets of downtown Deer Lodge, Montana were deserted. I could find no other place to wait for the tardy Limo driver who would haul me sixty the miles to catch my return flight from Airport at Helena, Montana's Capitol. I was forced to charm the reluctant proprietor with four bit tips and desperate conversation to keep him open until my ride arrived.

Had I stayed a teacher, I'd be luxuriously enjoying the Christmas hearth of some seriously unmarried girl's hopeful parents. I'm sure that parents of quickly maturing young spinsters, still consider a poorly paid English teacher adequately equipped to take over their daughter's support.

Hardin County's Sheriff Goodman had petulantly abandoned me at Chief's Bar. Probably, because I committed the flagrant sin of expressing my own opinions, while interviewing him for a story on the New Republic Revolt festering among some local ranchers. My mistake was assuming the Sheriff was a supporter of law enforcement and government taxation. I was mistaken. The targeted malcontents were all his relatives or on his Christmas Card list.

Most experienced reporters would have recognized Sheriff Elmo Goodman's anti-government sympathies and slanted thier reportage favorably toward that viewpoint. Then, Goodman might have assigned a deputy on his shit-list" to spend his holiday doing penance by driving me to the airport, instead of just giving me the phone number of a limo service. Goodman gloatingly said it was the same service he used to send stiffs to Helena for postmortems. Their drivers, I feared, were not usually expecting tips nor greatly concerned for passenger comfort.

Spouting Law and Order rhetoric had backfired with the Sheriff but that was what I thought he wanted to hear. Pandering to both opposing points of view was my usual tactic which allowed me write stories twice. Sometimes I could milk the same situation for three totally different stories, all from one set of interviews, and one expenses investment. A story on the opposing view, just required using a pseudonym.

My concern for suitable euphemisms and pen names was probably the reason I asked the bartender why the bar was called Chief's. My need for a warm place to wait for my ride had elicited no sympathy, but that question provoked a narrative that I hoped was long enough to stall his turning off his WELCOME sign, until my limo driver finally arrived.

The Bartender began, "Chief Joseph Deerhorn Hogan was a middle aged Indian, just released from Montana Penitentiary here at Deer Lodge Montana, three days early, and the day before Thanks-giving, forty-two years ago. Chief suspected those three days were more to reduce the number of inmates partaking of the expensive turkey and trimmings, than for compassion. Chief had served every day of the seven years, eight months and twenty-nine days of his ten year sentence for burglary, except those three days.

Without sponsor and as an destitute Indian, Joe was never seriously considered for parole. His non-violent and never completed burglary would have won him a bench parole, had he been more endowed with work record or a less dedicated drunk.

Waiting at the Bus Station, resplendent in new suit and topcoat from the prison tailor shop, he was the best dressed of the several people late starting home for the Holiday Weekend. He was richer than he had ever been holding four hundred dollars accumulated from his quarter an hour job in the license plate shop. His willingness to work hard without complaint had produced a job offer from a non-union metal fabrication plant in Flagstaff, Arizona. He was recommended by the prison's Warden, a reliable source of exploitable laborers for cost cutting employers.

Deciding that the Bus Depot was too institutional, Chief Joseph chose to spend the four hours of waiting for the Flagstaff across the street in The Silver Dollar Saloon. Hesitating about facing the honest citizens inside, Joseph Deerhorn, was bumped by another patron. She was an attractive young girl parodying a cowboy version of a dance hall gal. In spite of garishly done makeup and cheaply handsewn and recycled wardrobe, it was apparent that she was miscast in her role and obviously pregnant.

Chief Joseph, embarrassed at his clumsiness, backed into an elegant bow, and gallantly opened the door. The young girl introduced herself as Maggie, then propositioned him, but even Chief Joseph could tell that this whore was an amateur. Still, the inexperienced Indian agreed although had never slept with a woman, while sober.

After mutually inept negotiations, they made a date for supper and sex two hours later at her one room studio apartment over the Frontier Clothing store. Because Chief would not have to rent a hotel room, she asked him to bring a big bottle of something to drink, and two sandwiches.

Chief assumed she was desperate, hitting on him, as the thirty-four years of his life had not made him pretty. His face delineated his harsh life on an Indian Reservation and in a White Man's Prison.

Maggie said she was unemployed, fired as a waitress at the Bus Depot Coffee shop, when her coming baby, signaled its presence. Impoverished, and without friends, she stayed in Deer Lodge hopeful of winning a parole for her wished-for husband. Chief knew him as a fellow inmate named Clyde Wickshaw, who was a mean, incorrigible punk who had surrendered to easing his incarceration as both pervert and snitch. On Maggie's last visit, Clyde pleaded with her for fifty dollars to buy an early release. Broke and penniless, Maggie was determined to get the money.

That fifty might ease Wickshaw's suffering but it wouldn't

shorten his sentence. Saddened by her misplaced loyalty, Chief impulsively decided to stay in Deer Lodge long enough to get Maggie freed from the loser, Clyde Wickshaw.

After redeeming his ticket, Chief walked west on main street to Albert's 'always open' Supermarket. It was a long walk, out where the sidewalk ends at the fairgrounds and rodeo parking lot. Chief bought a large jug of cheap wine and spent fifty dollars on groceries, including a small turkey. He 'borrowed' the overladen shopping cart to wheel the food to Maggie's apartment.

Chief Joseph struggled through un-shoveled snow with the clumsy cart and because of several wrong turns from Maggie's confusing directions, was ten minutes late. Maggie was gone. He frantically searched for Maggie until he saw her note on the floor at the door.

Dear Joseph Deerhorn,

I sure hope you are only late and are reading this. You know how desperate I am to get the money for Clyde. When you did not come, I had to try getting money elsewhere. Goldy at Montana Gold and Pawn over on Hickory propositioned me today when I tried to pawn my earrings. He is a slime bag and I don"t trust him, so if I don't return by Ten, please tell someone. The door is unlocked as I have nothing to steal. Please come in and wait for me. I will understand if you won"t want me second-hand, but please wait to eat supper with me. I do have enough bread and eggs for both of us.

Chief's eyes watered. This was the first time anyone had written him a personal note and the first time anyone had used his real name. He did not remember telling Maggie his name. Chief had never had a real girl friend and had no one to work for or to love and protect. It was then, he adopted Maggie. Chief returned the store's cart, while planning their Christmas dinner and the night's snack. He had worked one year in the Prison kitchen and had been observant. Back at Maggie's, dinner was ready for the oven, and a kettle of soup was simmering, when Maggie returned. The pain of her encounter marked her tear streaked face. Chief's joy at hearing her footsteps on the stairs, turned to sorrow seeing the tears on Maggie's face. Chief impulsively opened wide his welcoming arms and Maggie first threw up her arms, defensively, before deciding to relax in the comfort of his embrace.

While she snuggled silently in his arms, Chief felt no need for a dismal confessional. He carefully picked up Maggie and laid her on the small bare, elevated on boxes, bed-raggled mattress she used as settee and bed. He covering her trembling body with his elegant new prison tailored overcoat, and watched her fall into deep sleep.

For the first time outside prison walls, Chief used his prison acquired writing skills to inventory the essentials Maggie's household required. He was certain his savings would cover their needs until he found a job. For the first time in his life Chief Joseph wanted, no required, a job.

Later, Chief brought Maggie the pan of soup and fresh squaw bread. Shaking her gently awake, he began spoon feeding his new charge. By the way she ravenously ate, Chief knew food had became a luxury and that accounted for her frailness. Finally full, Maggie dropped off again, still holding tightly to Chief's left hand, as he lay on the floor beside her bed. Awkward and cramped, Joseph could not sleep, and heard the furtive footsteps on the stairs, and was waiting when the unlocked door squeaked open.

A man snuck into the room and stopped, shocked at seeing Chief. Although the man had a gun in his hand, the momentary shock was long enough for the labor-hardened Indian to get one hand on the intruder's throat and the other on the wrist of the hand holding the gun. Many years of unloading sheet steel and feeding the blanking press at the license shop gave Joseph strength that the feebler pawnshop operator found overpowering.

Goldy squeezed out a plaintive cry of surrender through his

choked throat and realized he was seconds away from dying. The transition from threatening bully to whimpering coward left his brain numb and almost beyond revival before he realized that dropping the gun was his only chance of survival. That done, he felt himself lifted over the head of a very angry Indian Warrior who resonated with pent up angers.

Goldy felt relief, as he bounced down the stairs, content to be that far away, crippled or not. Powered by fear's alchemy, he struggled to his feet, swearing his visit was to bring more money for the earrings Maggie had pawned earlier. Chief Joseph, told him to leave the money at the foot of the stairs and to never get within arms reach of Maggie or himself. He did not feel it necessary to explain why. Joseph returned to Maggie, huddled under his overcoat and sobbing. Clumsily comforting her in arms unaccustomed to offering comfort or care, Joseph easily heard her pledge, repeatedly and resolutely though barely a whisper,'Never again. No man will hurt me, never again. Never again!'

Chief laid down again, uncomfortably sideways on the floor so he place his right hand, clasping hers, over her heart. Chief Joseph recognized the frantic beating of her heart just like that of a small rabbit he had chased and cornered in a hollow stump, twenty years ago. He did not let himself or anyone else hurt that rabbit nor would he allow harm to ever come to Maggie.

Despite the long years of court imposed chastity, Joseph refused Maggie's offering of physical reward, when she rolled of her crude bed, snuggling to him on the floor. Maggie refused to sleep, sharing with Joseph, her childhood. All of her hopes, her fears, her needs became Joseph's dominion. He confessed to her his few sins, admitting his attraction to alcoholic oblivion but pledged to never drink again because that might be the time she needed him most. He wanted to be Maggie's full time protector and friend. For ever, if she so desired.

Maggie told Chief that she wanted to love him always, they agreed to a sacred pledge, both holding on to the un-opened gallon jug of cheap port wine".

Reluctant to leave my shelter building snowstorm, I politely interrupted to, prolong the story, asking, "Did Joseph or Maggie ever open the wine?"

Interpreting my question as disbelief, the bartender turned to the back bar and opened a large cabinet above the assorted glassware. Opened, the door back, displayed a large photo. It was a picture of a mature Indian in full feathered headdress, helping a young white girl to mount a spotted horse. The only object in the cabinet is a somewhat dusty gallon jug of a common and inexpensive port wine. "You can see for yourself, the jug's seal is unbroken. This is their bottle," he said reverently.

"How do you know the story is true?" I asked, not to be skeptical, but to prolong the bartender's narrative, intending to ask questions until my ride arrived.

Assuming a pious air, the Bartender pledged, right hand held out, almost over an imaginary bible and swore in courtroom like manner, "My parents both told me the story many times, and it weren't one word different no matter when or who told it. And they didn't try to gloss over the embarrassing parts. If they were lying, they'd have prettified the story."

"You mean, you are that little baby, and Maggie is your Mother?"

"That first baby is Joe, Jr. He's a Lawyer. Works for the Indian Affairs Office in Washington, and has never set foot in this bar, or any other bar. Probably, the only teetotaler in the District of Columbia. Now me, I'm Woody. I'm the third and last of their siblings. I'm a writer, like you. At least, I was. Parents sent me to Missoula to study Journalism. After a few years of hard scrabble apprenticeship, they financed me to buy a partnership in a small daily in Idaho. Too much stress, and I took to drinking. Maggie came and got me one night, finding me more drunk than alive. Brought me here and gave me the bar. She said, "Drink yourself to death on your own booze, pissing away what your Father worked for eighteen years, double shifts, never drinking one drink. Spend your sober time thinking of the sweat, blood and tears he invested in this place to educate and feed you. Then drink it all up." And I haven't had a drink since."

"You said the place Chief and Maggie met was THE SILVER DOLLAR," I challenged, hoping for more story.

"This was the SILVER DOLLAR, but Chief changed it to MAGGIE"S JUG. Maggie made me change the name to honor Chief. He"d been dead almost a year when she came and got me. The name she chose was CHIEF"S BAR. Gave me that jug, and challenged, 'If I needed to drink, first drink the jug of consecrated wine so Chief and she saved it for nothing!' So there it sits, unopened. Oh, I drink a shot of colored water, once in a while when hospitality is forced upon me, but nothing alcoholic.. This bar has a real sobering history."

Right then, my driver arrived, and said we had to hurry as drifts are already closing main roads. I shushed him, holding up my right arm in the universal sign for "Hold on a minute!"

I turned to the bartender and asked,"Can I tell Chief's Story to the world?" and he just laughed as I followed the impatient chauffeur."

Later, in the limo as my driver turned off the main street onto Highway 2 toward Helena, he loosened his two clenched hand grip on the steering wheel, long enough to shake out a cigarette, and diverted my critical notice of his smoking, with a question, "You like your wait at Chief's bar? Did you know the owner is a genuine half-breed. A few years back, Indians couldn't buy liquor, and now they run bars."

DEACON STROPP'S PLEDGE

It was Thursday, and for Arnold Stropp, the best day of the week. His parts commission alone totaled almost two hundred dollars! It was his fifth day as Wilson Import Motor's most tenured employee and Arnie appreciated the privileges accorded the senior mechanic. Arnie moved his tools, lunch box and street clothes into the locker number one, vacated by Clarence Emberson. Clarence's AUDEL'S FOREIGN CAR MANUAL and his treasured Swiss micrometers cozily imbedded their custom cherry-wood tray and polished steel glory, remained forgotten on the top shelf.

Ann, the new cashier who, by default responsible for chores no one else wanted, cleared out the locker the day after Emberson's fatal heart attack. She gathered all of his shop possessions, and his final check and delivered them to his widow. Being quite short, Rita had not seen the valuable tools on the locker's top shelf.

Arnie now considered the manual and tools abandoned, and he the logical inheritor. He really didn't need the gauges, nor had Clarence used them other than to dazzle people with his technically superior measuring tools which were normally used just by machinists measuring critically accurate milling and grinding tolerances. Clarence had embarrassed Arnie for the last time, conning him into bets on gaps and fits, all shop employees in attendance, settled by measurement with his inviolate Swiss gauges. Arnie knew an antique dealer who would pay well for those tools. He would take that forgotten largesse there next week, unless someone from the Emberson family specifically requested their return.

Now as senior mechanic, Arnie would not be disputed on his interpretation of acceptable tolerance measures or his overtime decisions which upstart service writers had challenged. This last overheating Volvo, driven in by the vacationing dentist from Rhode Island, earned him another overtime hour today, but only because he had claimed he had
to wait for parts. For twenty years, he had sold water pumps to

people too dumb to realize a leaky radiator cap allowed water to boil at normal boiling temperature instead of the elevated pressurized temperature modern motors favored and their thermostats allowed.

Arnie took the Volvo's water pump into the customer lounge, and advised the worried looking but patiently waiting Doctor and his wife to authorize a new pump, and the extra hour labor charge, since resealing would be only a temporary fix. Arnie exuded sincerity and he confidently said, "Dr. Goldman, would you pull an infected tooth, repair it, but then put it back in? Now if you ever reinstall a failed component of a high performance automobile like your 970, your next breakdown could occur in a dangerous or in far from help spot." Seeing some hesitation, Arnie reached out, comfortingly, clasping the distraught doctor's forearm and trying a new tack, "I can get you a core credit of fifteen dollars for the old one. Would that help?" Implying they needed financial help always seemed to work when confronting successful people.

And the Doctor dutifully replied, "If that's the ransom it takes to get us out of here, put in the new one," then turned and mumbled something unintelligible to his wife.

As Arnie hoped, Dr. Goldman would not want to seem overly concerned with price, so Arnie had the Volvo's original for his home repair shop. Pleased, Arnie generously decided that he would forget whose people called for Christ's crucifixion and replace the faulty radiator cap secretly and for free since that would avoid revealing the real overheating problem.

"You ever come to Bergen New Jersey, you come see me. I will fix that misaligned incisor of yours, special! I appreciate you working late just to get me on the road, again," Doctor Goldman said clenching his right hand into a strong fist in his pocket, savoring a new thought. "I would love to get you in MY shop, and I would work overtime, too."

Arnie had been particularly pleased that he had guessed Dr. Goldman was a Dentist, and that his targeted victim was certainly not a Christian. His afternoon would be especially profitable and the near new Volvo water pump was easily worth two hundred dollars. Arnie liked being trusted, detesting suspicious customers, but Goldman's apparent awareness passed over Arnie's head.

Two weeks earlier, a lawyer with a two year old 190 Mercedes had accused him of contriving the emergency replacement of his car's alternator, insisting the OEM replacement offered was inferior and unnecessary. The Boy Scout Leader, senior service writer, had caved in and Arnie wound up re-installing the original alternator, and just replacing the stretched and slipping serpentine belt. Arnie lost his 20% commission on the four hundred dollar alternator and the rate book time of 1.2 hour which billed at half of the Fifty dollar hour shop rate. That naive service writer had cost him over a hundred dollars and many resultant dollars of profits for Wilson Import Moters. A few more surrenders like that and the timid service associate would be walking the streets.

Dan in parts, mocked Arnie, "You will sting a guy for a two hundred-fifty dollar water pump, than wimp out and donate a three dollar radiator cap. Arnie, I think you're turning soft because your buddy died.'

Dan did not realize the subtlety involved. Sell the Doctor a radiator cap, and he might just wonder whether if that alone was what caused his overheating. Dumb Dan with his big mouth didn't deserve any of the shop's profit sharing. Arnie did, and old man Wilson made more money from Arnie's parts replacement skills than from billing his repair time.

As senior mechanic and best on profits, he could have worked the desperate Goldman family for two hours overtime. He could have sold a radiator boil out, after the pump, blaming clogged radiator for the water pumps failure. It always told well, when he worked that ploy but he chaired a deacon's meeting at First Baptist at seven, and feared political machinations if all of the church leaders were assembled while he was not there. Arnie resented any challenges to his authority, veracity or piety.

Just enough time for Arnie to zip home and grab a quick sandwich and pick up his oldest son Tod. He had promised Tod, now newly licensed, that he could use Arnie's Mercedes while Arnie was at the Church. Lucky, his home was nearby in the core city, unlike most of Supreme Export Motors high priced mechanics, who all lived in the suburbs.

Arnie was enjoying his twenty minute paid cleanup time when he was paged. "You here, Arnie? Lady named Bea Larabee calling," said the impersonal voice on the intercom, and Arnie hurried to the closest phone, while mentally groping for an excuse to stall Miss Larabee again. He had forgotten his promise to finish her car today or call her before school closing. He picked up the phone, and assumed a very sad voice.

"Sorry Bea, thought I'd be calling you with good news, but I just found out your hydraulic percolator is bad. Your Power steering could fail while you're cruising down a highway and cause you to swerve into traffic or the ditch." Arnie's face reddened slightly, probably from seeing the open-mouthed stare of the watching parts man. "I know how bad you need the car, Bea. We don't stock percolators so I got to get one from the factory. I will check at home, tonight. Might have one I can...Just a minute Bea."Arnie covered the mouth piece while Lenny, the new parts man guffawed.

Brash and irreverent Lenny shouted to amuse the whole shop. "Anyone her ever hear of a hydraulic percolator? We'll have to stock them for Arnie's customers, if we find out what they are."

Still muffling the mouthpiece, Arnie continued, "Bea, I'll take one from my wife's car and get your car done tomorrow. I would get ticketed if I allowed you to drive the car the way it is. I've got to chair Church Council so I can't do it tonight. Sorry!" Bea had expected special consideration, as Arnie's junior year English teacher but had earned no favors with her stern attempts to polish his grammar. She had been the one teacher Arnie's football coach couldn't budge, attempting to get his star fullback special consideration and more lenient grading.

As neared home, he saw Tod; expectantly posted in the driveway, fearful his father had forgotten his promise and would be working late. It had happened before. Tod probably had helped his mother cook supper, so nothing would delay Tod's first car solo and important date. Just to tease, Arnie turned early and drove in the alley toward his five-car, backyard shop.

Inside his comfortable and spacious split level, everyone worked from the same play book. Arnold sat and surveyed his family gathered around the dining room table, already set with inviting food. His son Tod, daughter Ann, and wife Nora attentively waited on Arnold's rendition of the customary prayer. Nora, once a bouncy and extroverted cheerleader sat quietly deferential hoping her dinner efforts would be appreciated.

As usual, table-talk centered on Arnie's day and his interpretation of the divine blessings bestowed on him at his job, in his hometown while presiding summarily over the once small bungalow he had been born in. The house, like his first and only job, had been made more comfortable, renovated twice and was now three times its original size. It stood out, in stark contrast with the declining neighborhood, stark proof of Arnie's prosperity.

The whole town of Peaksville knew and deferred to Arnie and his God. Arnie had refused a tendered football scholarship at the State University, to stay with his admirers, and continue to serve them, while he continued to lust for their cheers. Nora, once a gregarious honor student, dutifully basked in her husband's glories, as penance for that prom night spent too long in the back seat of Arnie's old Ford. Their first born and somewhat early daughter Ann was the treasured compensation and her special child, somewhat neglected by her father.

Nora watched Ann listening courteously, not showing the strain of patriarchal subjugation which would drive her beautiful and beloved daughter away, soon as she graduated. Another year, they would both listen to Arnie with feigned attentiveness. Tod worshiped his father and emulated his every idiosyncrasy. It was he who fed the straight lines for Arnie's dinner time talks. Ann knew that Tod's compliant role earned him favored sibling role. The entrapment Nora or Arnie felt by Ann's early birth had not been a favoritism factor.

Nora remembered her hasty wedding, as the first of many times she had surrendered free choice. She dutifully returned her attention to Arnie's soliloquy. Nora silently watched Arnie eat without interrupting his chronicle of this day's accomplishments and ruefully remembered her mother's advice on picking a mate. "Watch him eat, while you ain't." she had said. Nora guessed her tolerance of his eating habits proved she still loved Arnie.

Finished with his favorite peach pie, Arnie reached in his pocket, fished out the keys to his almost new Mercedes and handed them to Tod. Immediately, the women were alone with so much to say and share, but both started clearing the table silently.

Tod drove carefully, exultant in his new role as a trusted and legitimate driver. His father silent, deep in thought about his strategy for the coming meeting, did not signal what he thought so Tod drove more carefully than he had for the driving inspector. At Union Baptist's stately but time-worn Cathedral, Arnie quickly jumped out, turned back and admonished his eager driver, "Be back here at ten-thirty, and waiting in the parking lot. No excuses! When I come out, you better be here!"

Arnie and Reverend Harlan Warland reached the council meeting room simultaneously, and Arnie beat the Pastor to the 'Bless you's'. This seemed an auspicious start for Arnie's agenda. He was worried about the role model sacrifice he would be expected to pledge. This was Arnie's first year as Chairman of the Stewardship Drive. Past Chairpersons usually pledged publicly and extravagantly, setting the tone for the other campaign workers, and indirectly, the rest of the congregation. Pastor Warland explained that job requirement after Arnie had agreed to serve. Harland knew his inner city congregation well, serving them for twenty years.

Halfway into the meeting, with all the campaign workers in attendance, the crises came. Reverend Harland abandoned his patient, behind the scenes role, urging the group, "We a're wrangling over a budget the trustees agonized over for many weeks, paring it to bare bones. There is no more fat to render. Mr. Chairman, to get us started on stewardship, I will tithe ten percent, this year. How about the rest of you on the management team?"

The moment Arnie feared had arrived! Since rashly agreeing to chair the Stewardship Committee, Arnie had sought rationale for his subdued charity. He explained, "because I believe sacrificial giving is that amount given secretly, and without recognition, I will only pledge ten dollars each week."Arnie, poised on the balls of his feet, and thought the silence was like game nights when he tensely waited for the quarterback's handoff. Just more quiet. He continued, "My important contribution will, as always, will be cash in the collection plate. A little pact I made with the Lord, reflecting his weekly blessings. He is my partner at work." Arnie piously beamed at the ceiling and hoped for is hopefully forgiving God. "However, most folks without such a contract with 'The Almighty' need fixed pledging, for our budgeting accuracy."

Again silence, "Now, if you all think I should publicize my stewardship as an example, I will double my pledge, but stop sharing my weekly financial blessings in the collection plate. Our finances will suffer since I put forty dollars in the plate last week."

Charles Lucassen, Church Treasurer, bit his tongue and remained seated and silent. Nothing would be served by saying, "If you put in forty dollars, Arnie, you contributed to at least four collection plates!" Lucassen wondered whether Harlan believed Arnie, which would be an accusation that he had siphoned off money, when he counted it and prepared the deposit slip. Surely, the minister had more faith in his summation of the offering. Charles had told the Pastor Warland, that the loose cash totaled fifty-nine dollars and twenty-three cents.

Seizing the moment, Reverend Warland quickly spoke, "Why, forty dollars a week is a truly magnificent pledge, Arnie. One few of the congregation will be able to match. Let's ask all of the council to emulate your fine example. I now have great optimism that our budget needs will be met. How about a cheer for our Stewardship Chairman, folks! We are blessed with his leadership."

Some embarrassing minutes later, outside in the cool autumn evening, Arnie still seethed. He had been snookered again by a master. Arnie was embarrassed to be still waiting at five minutes to eleven and moved to the shadows. Several friends had offered him a ride, not seeing his very noticeable car in the parking lot, when the meeting broke up at Ten-fifteen. Not wishing re-hashes of the evening's meeting, Arnie was glad to tell them his son was coming in a few minutes, and would not be late. He was, and Arnie alternated between worry and anger until almost eleven.

Arnie saw his car approaching down Carmen Avenue, two blocks north. He heard two tire screeching turns before his son arrived, now creeping to a stop before him. "Dad, I was so worried. You were standing in the shadows where I couldn't see you when I came by. I went by three times, and then decided you had caught a ride. I went almost home, before realizing that when you said here in the parking lot, that was where I should wait."

"Two words for you, Tod," he angrily shouted. "You are a liar!" He jerked open the driver's door and snatched the keys from the ignition. "You've earned the right to walk home, but first, you go into the church, get down on your knees before the altar and beg forgiveness for your lies. Remember Christ told Moses to honor your Father and Mother that your days may be long. That sacred fifth commandment means always telling your Dad the truth. I can understand being late, but not deliberate lying to your father!"

DEVLIN'S OFFER

Paul Foss, Vice-President of Globe Pharmaceuticals, New Product Development, normally left work right behind his secretary yet he had not moved from his cozy and ergonomically-correct swivel chair since she left at four. Deep in troubled thought, he resented the ominous ring coming in on his private phone line. No one should expect to find him here, and only a select few people knew his number. A security device screened out all but those persons entitled to access him on that unmonitored, transcription-free line. Irritated, but curious, Paul moved for the first time since beginning his pensive but non-productive trance.

Paul pushed the speaker button and heard a rich, resonant bass voice he did not recognize but of tone and timbre he had longed to acquire. With slow and dramatic articulation, the voice said, "Working late, Paul? That's not like you at all."

Paul was baffled. He considered which of his intimates were capable of alterining their voice in such a manner, and how they would know he stayed late. Was it a prank or some malicious machination from the game politic, played so prevalently among the more ambitious junior executives? Paul was sure he had grown above that rank, having played the game well, but not lately.

Deciding that no answer was the wrong response, he spoke, choosing words very carefully, "Who are you? And what the Hell are you doing on my private line?"

"Why, I'm your good friend and patron, Sanford Devlin, but we have not yet met. I am concerned with your problem. The Executive Board is expecting you to present a new miracle drug's particulars at ten tomorrow and you have nothing. Or can you see some magic formulae on that blank piece of paper in front of you?"

Paul"s eyes shot to his office's outer glass wall, and realized the secure kevlar drapes were closed, blocking light, electrons or even bullets from penetrating. Reassured, he determined to unravel the identity of the mystery speaker and to divine his motive. He would keep Deeman speaking and with adroit questioning, assess his caller's motives. "So, Mr. Devlin, how did you get my name and number?"

"You mustn't be suspicious, Paul. I just dialed the right numbers, and presto, there you are. Remember, it is you that promised something you can't deliver, not me. When you are on fire and someone arrives with a bucket of water, should you ask him who he is or where the water came from?"

"Globe Pharmaceuticals is the World's third largest drug company and mainly, because of my leadership. They were only fifth, when I became director of research," Paul said, while wishing for some current corroboration of that capability.   "And just what miraculous new drug has your direction inspired," Devlin said with elegant sarcasm.

"I developed the top selling anti-inflamation drug, and the second-best appetite suppressant," Paul exulted.

"Come off it Paul, tell that to TIME. We both know that your predecessor, Hanson developed Fevrid", but was holding it until the issue of stomach lining necropsy was pursued further. He went into the board meeting with nothing because you set him up. Neat work, Paul. Carl Hanson was your friend, and I didn't think you would pull it off."

"I only thought he was my friend. He was chasing my wife. I only retaliated, and Carl came up loser."

"You only thought you fooled Carl and your long-suffering wife, Madge, with your crazy allegations. Well, not crazy, because your strategy did work, unless you wanted to keep your wife and kids. Madge was bright and figured your wild rampage was to justify betrayal of your friend. Hanson may have even believed you thought him capable of cuckolding his best friend and assistant, but I knew better, and so did Madge. She knew you set up that phony clandestine meeting as neither of them did."

"So, you are a blackmailer. She's gone. Both kids are gone, what do I have to lose. Carl cut his wrists. How can a cheap blackmailer like you, hurt me?"

"Blackmailer? Maybe, once in a while, but cheap, never. I did not accumulate billions without using wiles and some questionable tactics, but even I wouldn't have planted the offer from Provident Drugs sent to you, in Hanson's desk. You convinced the board that Carl was holding back Fevrid for them. That was an evil betrayal done masterfully."

"Only the President of Provident knew who that offer was really directed to, Devlin. He would not dare let you use that information to blackmail me, unless he wanted to do serious jail time. Tell him that I know you are bluffing, and though I might get hurt, he would go to jail, because I never sent the formula."

"My esteem for you is declining, Paul. You are so reactionary. Focus on the meeting, tomorrow. What do you want to tell the board? Do you want to deliver what you promised? I quote your words, 'Something spectacular that could possibly shift Global into the number one pharmaceutical company in the World!' Right? Wouldn't you like to talk about something so overwhelmingly saleable, that your pitifully meager past accomplishments, would be overlooked? Something that would have them clamoring to make you their President, or even CEO?"

"So what would this little miracle cost me, Mr. Devlin? My soul? Are you just setting me up?"

"Paul, you are the proven master of the set-up. I just want you to be my partner in the biggest financial coup since Teapot Dome. This is not Faust. This is you and I controlling the biggest company in the World."

"Your hyperbole sounds too good to be true. I should agree just to watch you fall on your face."

"Now, you sound like the reasonable executive I judged you to be. Meet me in the executive lounge room in two minutes."

"We can't! That"s set up on auto lock. Our President himself couldn't get in there, now. We would be taped with camera surveillance, if we could get in."

"Meet me there in two minutes. The camera won"t be

working and the door will be unlocked."

Skeptically, Paul pushed open the free swinging door to the executive lounge and cautiously stepped in. Devlin, or somebody had turned on the lights but nobody was there. Paul heard splashing sounds from the attached men"s room. Then he, he heard, Devlin's stentorian voice rumbling. "Hello Paul, I'm in here. I needt to stay in the stall, until we have mutual commitment. You do not see my face if until we are partners."

"Are you proposing we do something illegal, or so shameful that you must hide your identity? You must have been recorded somewhere in this security first building."

Devlin, apparently unable to speak in soft, confidential tones, answered in his loud, forceful manner, "My voice cannot be taped. Remember, I am proposing that you become the richest man in the world. Croesus would seem a comparative beggar. If you are interested, enter the first stall, and sit,"

Whether from the hypnotic quality of Devlin's voice or the prospect of getting rich, Paul quickly complied. He entered the stall, lowered the gold trimmed mahogany cover, turned and sat down. Seconds passed before Deeman began. "Do not interrupt me with questions. Listen carefully for I will not repeat myself. When I ask you, yes or no, you can answer only one word. If it is no, leave and don't look back. If yes, I will be your silent partner and I will place fifty million dollars in your brokerage account, and direct you to perform your duties, by my direction. You will wear in your ear an audio instrument that is now setting on your desk. Tomorrow, you will explain to your colleagues, that you have discovered and corrected a small hearing loss. Through that device, I will monitor your words and communicate with you. Before your board meeting tomorrow, call your broker, instructing him to purchase up to one million Globe shares, when it reaches ten dollars less than yesterday's closing. Then, you announce at the board meeting, that you have both good news and bad news, to report. Someone you have met wants to purchase controlling interest in Globe Pharmaceuticals and proposes to buy any of their shares at two dollars more than Thursday noon's closing price."

"You are certifiably crazy, Devlin. Why would our directors sell at three dollars premium? I certainly would not!"

"Paul! You interrupted despite my instructions. Hear the bad news. Very soon, we, that's you and I, will set in motion a terrible downward slide in Globes value that the directors will all justifiably fear has no bottom. Only when we have a full majority, will we correct that downward dip. The downward slide will be triggered by your announcement of resignation because of a pending indictment for price fixing. You are volunteering to be the sacrificial lamb, rather than risk taking the other officers and directors down with you."

"I'm not guilty of price fixing, and not under indictment. Why would I say..."

"There you go again, Paul. Giving me today's news. Tomorrow is another day and the day after, you will have your indictment. A propitious indictment that will help you become the richest man in the world. If you keep interrupting me before I ask a question, I may change my choice of you as partner. Your associates will not feel pity at your pending indictment, nor grateful for your sacrifice. Many would ride out the dip in stock value you have precipitated, remembering the kind past. But none of them will savor any investigation of them for illegal insider trading practices. They will dump their holdings and run. You will be exonerated only when it is to our advantage. Any questions?"

"How the Hell, will you stop the slide, once it is started? I don't have new product. If I did, I wouldn't be listening to you.."

"Last chance to be rich, Foss," still speaking in a loud, hypnotic voice, but just a little less presumptive, "Do I have your attention. I have a formula in my hand for you to present to the board, and they will think it is an unproved cure for a disease that doesn't exist. It is a skin potion that will not require FDA approval.

Yet, in six months, after we own Globe, it will be the most profitable medicine ever produced. No one but me, can supply the one active ingredient, so there will not be a generic match. It is simple and inexpensive to produce. It is the only germicide that will halt the growth of a dreadfully virulent bacterial infection that's now invading human bodies."

Endless seconds passed, Paul's voice would not leave his throat, finally Devlin broke the silence. "Now, if we are partners, reach down and pick up the formula that I drop on the floor. I give you three minutes before I am gone the way I came, and you can face the board empty-handed, plus the coming collusion charge."

Paul assayed Devlin's words. If they were nothing but a crazy man's ravings, how dangerous could it be. He picked up the piece of paper, and held it up to read. He heard splashing in the adjoining stall, but continued reading

Congratulations! You are now contaminated with my special actinomycete! We are now partners. Don't bother washing your hands, as it will not wash-off. It is not life threatening, only disfiguring, like leprosy. You will be able to keep it in check with daily application of Globe"s new skin lotion. It will be terribly expensive, but as my partner, you will easily be able to afford it.

People who haven't the money will suffer disfiguring purple and hairy growths, wherever their hands touched. Untreated disfigurements will eventually drop off, but so wills the afflicted part. Be sure you shake everyone's hand as you bid them farewell, tomorrow. I will bring you a week supply of that secret ingredient tomorrow night, along with our game plan. Don't try to analyze this substance as that will break down its chemical bonds, leaving only sulphur, carbon and a trace of nitrogen. Just mix the ingredient with any hand lotion. It will not kill the bacteria, but does keep it in check. I will not prevent contagion to those you touch. We will talk again tomorrow. Wait in the hallway outside your private office, tomorrow evening at 7:00 P.M.

Paul watched incredulously as the note he finished reading turned into a wet soggy mass of toilet tissue. Paul stood up banged his door open and pulled open the door of the adjoining stall but found it empty. Empty, except for a gigantic black animal with a long rat-like tail that was miraculously squeezing its disgusting bulk down the much smaller opening in the accommodating commode. Paul shrieked the first of ten thousand screams that he would scream that last day he spent at Globe Pharmaceuticals.

Midge, Paul's niece and secretary, exited the parking garage and tolerantly held her electronic key toward the security guard before entering the secured elevators but was stopped and summoned over to the entry guard"s desk. A bother she did not want. Her sleep-over guest had caused delays that fast driving did not overcome, and she was nearly ten minutes late. Paul, her perplexing boss was finicky about tardiness, except for himself. As she had screeched in, she noticed Paul's yellowish green, Porsche Boxer parked in his stall. Even if it were the corporate color of Globe, no one else would demonstrate their bad taste, painting such a beautiful car the shade of fresh snot. She would suffer Paul's snide lecture on tardiness, so a little butt-chewing from an officious, poorly paid security guard, shouldn't matter.

Choosing to use charm, she turned, demurely, curtsied deeply exposing decolletage, and sweetly said, "Yes Officer, you want to check me or my card?" and extended her security card toward the blushing and overly cautious, guard.

Not reaching for the card, he asked in hushed and conspiratorial tone, "Didn't you hear what happened to your boss, last night? I didn't want you shocked. The cleaning crew found him sitting at his desk, in a pool of blood. Mr. Foss had cut off the fingertips of his left hand and he was trying to do the same to his right hand with a knife clenched in his teeth. I was here when the cops hauled him to Bellevue. He kept trying to tell them it was all the Devil's fault. See! Over by the elevator, that blood pool. Paul stood there while the cops secured the elevator. It was pouring out of his fingers. I just didn't want you to be shocked. The cleaning crew had to leave with the cops, so the all of his office is still a bloody mess."

BITS & PIECES OF DEATH
At twenty, I danced with death and found
impermanence disturbing. When again sound
and healthy, I reluctantly pondered how
my postponed death should come, and now
I'm far too sane and cowardly to crave
the pain that buys a hero's hallowed grave.
I favor calm ambush of death in sleep,
but not until I'm old and bored. I keep
enjoying death deferred in bits and pieces.
Supplies of forged body parts increases
while their need, I reluctant realize.
Although I mourn as my body dies,
it's less of me, more of technology.
Dying piece by piece now seems to me
the ideal way to go. As they excise
my worn out parts, replacements do suffice.
With death delayed by using proxy parts,
who can tell when my funerary starts.
I know and grasp an increasing degree
of death. When they finally agree
that most of me has stopped and gone,
what remains? Will part of me continue on?

FICKLE TIME

The cloudless Arizona sky gave little hint of the growing wind, but Carl Onsgard felt the sideways thrust on his steering wheel. He stopped to check his tires and was startled by an inquisitive jackrabbit, dashing by, pushed even faster by desert wind of deceptive strength. Not yet high noon but that western gale was searing hot. Finding no tires flattened, Carl hurriedly returned to the air-conditioned comfort of his rental Lincoln. Before starting, he checked his complimentary Hertz map. His yellow high liner had earlier marked the twisted itinerary that led to his appointment, the secluded mountain resort of San Jacinto.

Aware of the wind, Carl resumed driving, just a bit more carefully and ten minutes later he saw the San Jacinto exit sign of state road 45. Carl figured he had less than an hour's drive remaining, leaving more than adequate rest and preparation time. Despite Flight 239's hour take-off delay at New York's Kennedy and the slowing head winds toward Phoenix, he could still squeeze in a needed hour's nap before the big meeting. The past week"s regimen of eighteen hour days had allowed little sleep, straining Carl"s mental acuities. Carl obsessed with developing a simple yet understandable rationale for his revolutionary Onsgard Hypothesis, drained his body and brain.

No one but the President of the United States could impose such a rigorous undertaking on such short notice, and he had. The President asked Carl to assemble and lead the nation's best energy experts in a quest of energy sources, less dangerous than conventional nuclear plants and cleaner than the conventional ozone layer depleting coal-fired steam generators. Carl surmised he was chosen because he 'almost' had the answer.

Either the President believed the gap between almost and fait accompli was small, or was gamely trying to honor an overoptimistic campaign promise to create clean energy. Naming Carl to spearhead that group would be the first public recognition of Carl's efforts. A full lifetime of dedicated research had brought Carl to the brink of solving the unsolvable. Only the most brilliant of his science community peers recognized Carl's eminence in cosmology and nuclear physics, or cared. Carl who could not imagine how the President even knew his name.

Pushed by the strong wind tailing wind while absent-mindedly concentrating on the remaining riddle of plasma containment, his speed increased, dangerously. Ahead, the road was smoothly tarred though narrow and twisting but with no traffic. Carl thought this could not be the best or usual route to the tony, high-bucks dude ranch where Carl would preside over his compatriots in the week long symposium, as he met little traffic.

All those nominees he had listed for the President were brilliant scientists and Carl doubted his ability to captivate with nothing but an Aalmost" solution. Carl tried to wipe clean the virtual blackboard that always existed in his mind, to fully concentrate on strategies for presenting his theories in the most favorable and inspiring manner.

Jolted to attention by the car tires protesting screech, he read the Lincoln"s speedometer. It now indicated eighty-five which, much too fast for the narrow and twisting road. Slowing slightly, he became aware of more jackrabbits which, when studied closely, turned out to be swirling sagebrush bunnies chased across the road by the desert storm.

Suddenly, the sky darkened, not from rain, but sand. He slowed to a crawl, aware of and fearing the steep inclines on alternating sides of the rapidly ascending and twisted road. Carl saw a sudden pair of headlights coming straight at him and instantly swerved to the right. The Lincoln's outside wheels slid off the macadamized road, finding a treacherous patch of loose sand. A large semi or bus sped by, narrowly missing Carl"s side-wise skidding sedan. A thin millimeter to the left was a five hundred feet deep ravine.

Immediately, the sand storm abated as if sucked along with that passing vehicle. The dark cloud lifted and the road ran straight and flat. Carl was now on a broad treed mesa and the sun was again shining reassuringly bright with a clear blue sky background. There was no sign of wind and not another car in sight. The tension of the near miss triggered a searing pain in his forehead, triggering an explosion of light that seared his optical nerves and scorched an image in his cerebellum.

The ever present blackboard in his brain now displayed his familiar calculus proof, just as he had left it chalked on his Princeton lecture hall, except this theorem was complete. The lightning in his brain had apparently brought him the long solution he had dedicated his life to finding. Fusion is containable. A resolution so simple, yet previously unthinkable, startled Carl with its simplicity. He jammed on the brakes and wrote the revelatory but slight variation in Van Planck"s Constant in his always present, pocket sized note book.

All physicists since Bethe had incorrectly used an absolute. Confidently whistling his and Einstien's favorite Ode to Joy, and Carl could hardly wait to amaze his peers with his new insight. He now had the key Fermi and Bohr had overlooked.

Jubilantly resuming his drive, Carl was nearing a small town with trees and scattered buildings. He noticed a gas station on the town"s outskirts and compulsively decided to check whether the car needed attention after encountering that brief but lusty sandstorm. The town limits displayed a sign proclaiming that 399 happy people live in Salida Crossing.

Pulled in at the pump, he was greeted by an eager young attendant, with an engaging grin who cheerfully enquired, "Fill er up, Sir?"

He nodded and hoped the station offered full service as the windshield, now seemed quite dirty. He presumed dust from the sandstorm but learned different from the attendant, who said, "I'll check the oil and clean your windshield but the glass looks hazy because it has been sand-blasted. I'd suggest changing oil and the filters on your car before going any farther. Takes but an hour."

Not wishing to risk breakdown that would delay his arrival at the Symposium and his grand moment shocking the scientific world, Carl decided to gamble that Hertz would reimburse him. Yes, do what ever it needs. If your scamming me, your doing it with a nice smile." He jubilantly checked his watch, noting it was only 12:10. "Any place I can stretch a cup of coffee out for an hour?"

The friendly attendant pointed down the street along the side of the station, "Try the Diner down a block. Great coffee and the homemade pie is even better!" The diner was visible and a pleasant walk. He passed several slightly dilapidated houses on the way, but they seemed empty. Several people were eating in the Blue Plate Diner and across the street and down a block, several people were sitting on a bench in front of a very old building that obviously had once been a railway station but he saw no tracks and none apparent in his drive through the countryside. A someway functional remnant of the past, he surmised.

At the diner counter, he ordered a cup of coffee from a pretty freckle-faced young girl, with long, pale white hair. "Just a little cream," he added and then asked, "Let me know when it is one o'clock, please."

Carl watched her give him a long, puzzled stare, before she incredulously said, "It is already three-thirty by my watch, same time as they broadcast on the radio."

Carl looked again at his watch and it still said twelve ten, although the second hand was revolving in its usual manner. Puzzled, he looked for a clock on a wall, and saw a sign warning, "No breakfast served after Ten AM," but an older man at the counter was eating freshly served pancakes and eggs, while next to him, a young kid in a black motorcycle jacket was wolfing down spaghetti like he worked all day without lunching.

Amazed, Carl pondered explanations, while apprehensively checking his notebook where he thought he had transcribed his invaluable discovery. Aberrant clocks were less important. Making sure that his sudden insightful flash still existed, and would make sense on his eventually deciphered computer became the most important event in his whole lifetime.

He found the new revelation still recorded in his notebook. The solution was so very simple! His often discredited and mocked search for controlled fusion was now complete. Finally, justification for his lonely and reclusive existence. The impossible dream would bear his name. Electricity would be generated by slow, controlled fusion of hydrogen into helium. Cheap and non-polluting electricity would end food shortages, eliminate need for war and make life on Earth, a paradise.

The disconcerting explanation for his stalled watch came from the radio previously playing softly above the grill. In sudden loud volume, it blared. "Arizona Highway Officials announced that Carl Onsgard, brilliant Nuclear Physicist and one of few Cosmologists going beyond Einstein's theory of Relativity, perished in a one car accident in the rugged San Jacinto Mountains of Arizona. Witnesses said his car plunged down a steep embankment during a sudden blinding sandstorm. The truck driver who witnessed the accident said Onsgard ran swerved off the road just past noon. More details, next hour."

Carl laid five dollars by his half-filled cup of coffee and bolted into the street, bolting toward the lone service station where he had left his car. He would leave his precious pocket notebook to be found in his rented car. Recognition of his efforts would come.

Carl's iridescent, dark green Lincoln was parked beside the station, but the front end was elevated by a bright red wrecker, and he could see from a block away, that the Lincoln's front end was demolished and the cracked and bulged out windshield was stained with apparently his blood. If he could but walk back to the car with his priceless discovery, his name would live forever.

Streets in Salida are all one way, and he could not return. A far off plaintive train whistle, startled Carl. More people were in the street and were all heading toward the old building that had once been a Railway Station, at the end of the street. Everyone walked toward the station, and no one was walking the other way. The old man from the Diner had abandoned his cakes and was walking beside Carl and asked, politely, "You have the time, Sir?"

Looking again his watch, and noting for the first time, the crystal was blood-stained and severely scratched, barely allowing him to see the hands. They still indicated Twelve-ten. Carl realized that his solved equation would not ever be published in any worldly journal and he, like maybe the others with him in the crowded street had their most pressing puzzles answered but only when they had ran out of time.

SOMETHING FISHY ON MY PLATE

A fresh brook trout is pricy treat,
sautéed by Chefs before it's dead
Then served, full dressed, for you to eat
with baleful eyes still in its head.

I may be crude, to not eat trout
when it expires while being cooked
with crusted sneer upon its snout,
from tortured lips where it was hooked.

A Chef might laud this oppressed dish,

but I believe it ranks obscene

To pay surcharge for half dressed fish

that no one cared to even clean.

GOLDY'S LAST GOOSE

Bill Seeger sliced the home made bread carefully cutting two very even slices but leaving a thick heel for his longtime friend and hunting companion. Goldy lay expectantly at his feet but lifted her head from his foot and fixed her cataract clouding but still softly beseeching eyes on Bill, confident he would supply all her needs. Her graying and ragged coat no longer would inspire anyone to name her Goldy but sixteen years earlier, she had been pick of the litter with lustrous golden hair and flashing hazel eyes.

Seeger and Goldy had both aged considerably since their last birthday. When Bill dropped the crusty heel slice to Goldy, he noticed the back of his left hand had a large new liver spot. Yes, he too, was getting old. Bill carefully placed his two slices in the toaster warily setting the knob to just short of dark. Bill could not risk wasting the last of the double batch of seven grain butter-crust bread, Madge had baked for the freezer, the night before she learned her miserating and detested chemotherapy had to be resumed.

Grown used to Madge's home baking during the forty-eight, almost perfect years of marriage, Bill did not care for store bread nor wish to bake his own. Not that he couldn't but that might desecrate her memory. He just would not eat bread, when hers was gone. Bill quickly rinsed the coffee pot, his cup and his cereal bowl, noting that Goldy had relished every drop of the usual remainder of milk and bran flakes he always left for her, and the kitchen remained spotless. Sharing the left over cereal with Goldy had became their ritual once their son Dean married and left home. Dean had an unshakeable mental block about eating from dishes dogs had ever used and would wipe each clean bowl that might have been used to feed Goldie, over again on his dirty jeans or tee shirt. Their daughter, Nancy was less squeamish about dogs but shuddered when anyone touched her silverware.

Bill hoped both his children would understand why he and Goldy chose today. The late October clouds hung snow-gray and low, creating somberness that neither he nor Goldy felt. Bill had hinted at his reason for choosing today in letters to both children casually pinned to the bulletin board, stamped and ready for mailing. Bill had simply said that he and Goldy were no longer capable of the rigors of their long cherished goose hunting expeditions and this outing would be their last. He had not mentioned this day was exactly two months since Marge had gone. Their last days together had passed so quickly.

It was taking far longer for their "hunter's breakfast" than on their last outing two years ago when they were both younger and less crippled with arthritis. Bill ate breakfast alone during hunting season as Madge, protesting against killing of animals or avoiding intrusion into his and Goldy's favorite activity, slept late. It was only those mornings she had not prepared breakfast for everyone before waking the rest of the family.

Bill wondered what magical alarm clock she used to quietly wake without rousing her surviving loved ones and hoped he would remember to ask her. Groping in his old worn hunting jacket Bill found the old truck's keys and the one inch diameter cork that would just squeeze in the hole he had already shot in the bottom of his duck boat, in preparation for today's hunt.

Standing slowly, his arthritic knees stiff and slow to loosen, he unobtrusively pulled on Goldy's collar, helping her to stand. Goldy was sensitive about needing help. Without speaking but with mutual accord they went to the driveway where his painstakingly restored old Ford pickup, now promised to Nancy's fourteen-year-old son Jason, was parked. The punctured duck boat was already loaded, ready to go. He had filled the truck's gas tank, so there was enough for the trip to Hanson's Great Swamp, and for its eventual delivery to Nancy's house in Fargo.

Bill had almost forgotten shells for the old reliable Remington twelve-gauge shotgun designated for Dean, who didn't hunt but would probably display it on the wall of his den. Hopefully, Dean would see the gun as symbol of his father's joy and happiness, and not a macabre reminder.

Too bad, Dean's wife didn't tolerate dogs in their fancy home, he thought, wistfully forgetting that any days left to Goldy would be increasingly plagued with pain. Bill opened the passenger door, and unobtrusively as possible, helped his beloved retriever into the cab knowing this would be the last time she must suffer the ignominy of being boosted aboard.

The ride to the swamp was so familiar, Bill could drive it in his sleep. He was, however, seeing those oft traveled streets and roads differently, for the first time noticing the beauty of nature contrasted with the ugliness of careless or greedy men. Mankato had always seemed a friendly town to both Bill and Marge and he passed several spots they had mutually enjoyed. Madge loved the old river road that meandered north to Nicollet, where she taught school the first four years of their marriage, while he was still working part time at the Free Press, and attending Mankato State.

They had enjoyed several grand picnics at Riverbend Park, when they both lacked money for more expensive dining. Bill slowed to see if the now condemned band pavilion was still there, a decrepit but marvelous monument to their first kiss. Bill somewhat relished the realization that both he and Madge would be gone before the old pavilion was finally down.

On hunting trips to Swan Lake, Goldy insisted on having the window on her side of the cab down, no matter how frosty the fall air. Her marvelous nose traced their route, enabling her to start stretching before they turned down Orchard Road, to their favorite launching spot. Today, she lay on the seat with her head lightly on his lap, not caring to taste the crisp fall wind.

Bill worried why she seemed apprehensive, then realized he had not loaded the usual gunny sack and cooler for the birds.

Goldy must have realized that Bill did not plan to bring any geese or their detritus home. That realization did not seem to bother her too much as Bill was sure she was comforting him with her reassuring chin on his lap.

Another hour later, they were afloat in the boat, the new dawn signaling the opening of the season. The cork was securely placed in the hole already shot in the bottom of their boat. They heard one or two impatient hunter's premature shots and Goldy's heart was pumping adrenalin, overcoming the pain of her crippling rheumatism. She carefully moved rearward against the stern, eager to fulfill again her instinctive destiny as her master's hunting companion and aide.

They were in the very middle of the swamp, where the waters were cold and deep with the shoreline three-hundred yards away. Bill took his right-hand glove off with his teeth and then pulled at the cork set in the twelve-gauge hole in the bottom of the boat while stroking Goldy''s head with his other hand. The loosely fit cork would not come free, probably snagged by the rough edges of the hole, or maybe caused by his subliminal fear of being judged a quitter. Just because Madge had not taken any short cut away from her suffering, did not make Bill's decision wrong. Ending their days here was the right solution for he and Goldy yet the cork resisted his efforts to pull it out and flood the boat.

Almost striking him, a giant snow goose took to the air from nowhere. Bill watched in awe as the beautiful bird circled. Where was its flock? Geese never travel singly, and yet, there it was, boldly daring him to shoot while it completed a full circle, well within gun range.

Bill remembered stories of newly widowed geese, always mated for life, repeatedly buzzing hunters until they too, drew fire and were mortally wounded. The pure white goose buzzed him again, even lower. Like him, was it seeking respite from the heartache of a lost mate? His mind puzzled with what similarity made this beautiful goose seem so familiar. Goldy too, excitedly jumped onto the seat by him, she too seeing familiarity. Bill did not want to shoot the noble trophy but destiny declared he must.

The solitary white goose, radiant in the new dawn, Wheeled and slowly, more deliberately flew straight at him. Billstood, pointed and fired. The magnificent bird stopped still in mid air, then plummeted into the water beside them. Goldy, miraculously energized, sprang over the side while Bill clumsily rose to stabilize the boat. The duck boat capsized.

They were together in the icy water and Goldy, always infallible, did not have the bird and it was nowhere to be seen. Bill was treading water, aware that he could not survive long in his hunting gear, but was reluctant to be found partially undressed. He had not brought the required preserver seat cushions as he had not planned to want them. Bill was aware of Goldy struggling to pull him to shore by his sleeve but the numbing cold was dulling even his concern for her pain. Surely, Goldy understood the true purpose of their trip and would not torture her body with life-saving effort. The great white goose had made the sinful decision for both of them, absolving him from guilt, especially of making that cowardly decision for Goldy.

When hunters found them, dog and master lay together on the muddy bank with Bill's hand clutching Goldy's collar and her jaws still locked on his sleeve. Bill and Goldy were both smiling, and at peace.

HER CHOCOLATE KISSES

Betty wiped the fog from the bathroom mirror, and surveyed her fifty-year-old torso critically through nearly closed lashes. Maybe another three or four years, she would be able to keep up with her sisters at Freddy's. Then she would shed her bunny suit and petition the Austin School Board for recognition of her not expired teacher's certificate. She cupped her hands below each breast, lifting and shaping the cleavage her scanty, sequined bustier would present. They were young and well formed.

Her last boy friend likened them to a pair of large strawberries bobbing in cream. It was then she noticed that the berry on the left felt warmer. Her nightly hot flashes, trapped more by her folded arm, she was sure. Confidently she stepped, still damp from the shower, to her unflinchingly honest and extremely accurate clinical scale. She was pleased to see she was still two pounds under her targeted one hundred and thirty pounds, and gleefully rewarded herself with two chocolate kisses from the dish on the scale's indicator arm.

It would be proper to re-weigh after a second exercise routine and the possibility of winning three more chocolates, fueled her zeal as she began with her deep knee bends. At the re-weighing, she earned the hoped for three kisses and let them slowly melt in her mouth while she dressed. Her appointment with Dr. Mellor was in less than one hour so there was no time for a second shower, even if somewhat needed. Dr. Mellor, an old school Gynecologist over seventy, would not be distracted by a few stray pheromones, she rationalized, but Betty was more lavish than usual with her Dark Sin cologne.

Betty did have a date with one of last night's nicer customers whose sloppily dressed appearance seemed to confirm his claim of bachelor status. She had agreed to a meet him after her appointment with the Doctor. His name was Tom Sherbett, and she had found his name listed in the city directory, just as he claimed.

While rummaging naked through her closet, she did remember that she forgot to close the window. Often, when the window and shade were up for night ventilation, she forgot to close them. Now, she was deliberate. That friendly widower with the big smile and gorgeous blue eyes had moved in directly across the courtyard and often sat at his window. They were mutually aware of the courtyard scenery. A little extra pirouette for his greedy eyes, and her confidence was restored.

Betty had not realized she was always a bit of an exhibitionist, and reveled at that discovery. Strange morality, she mused. If that man watching were caught, he would be guilty of voyeurism. Yet, if she were to watch him display his equal disregard for modesty, he would again be guilty but of criminal exhibitionism. Betty stretched voluptuously for her phantom peeper, and rejoiced at being unwrinkled and trim. From that distance, he couldn't see the liberal freckling that was inevitable with redheads, nor detect the encroaching gray hairs she punished with hair tint.

Betty waited at the curb for the bus, electing not to drive, as she was planning a few drinks with her luncheon date. Dates for lunch got off easily, and she felt no guilt over ordering large on the reduced price lunch menu. She was not a big eater but did appreciate bringing home a "doggy bag" with a left-over portion of the meat entree to replenish her perpetually simmering crock pot. The complimentary vegetables in that one dish meal were inexpensive and well within her budget. Coupled with paper plates and plastic silverware, she had no need for a kitchen and was comfortable in her studio apartment.

Because she would meet Tom at the club, she was hopeful Tom would offer to drive her home. Betty hated the subterfuge of pretending not to have a car while it sat building up extra parking charges. Groping in her pocket for the bus fare, she found a single M&M, strangely uneaten during the coat"s last wearing, the previous night.

Betty wondered what color it would be. Only if it were red, would she not eat it. Since celebrating the first half-century of her life, last year her memory seemed to be deteriorating and she wondered whether the neglected candy left over from the reward she allowed herself for not sneaking any drinks, during her shift last night at Freddy's. No, she had consumed her chocolate self reward at the end of her shift, although she had been forced to consume two drinks. The first, a martini that Rick, her favorite bartender, told her to pour out as it should have been vodka. The second, an over sour martini that Manny, the crabbier senior bartender insisted she pay for. Manny said the error was hers, so that justified making a long-time and popular waitress responsible for every drink served.

Looking in her hand, she was exultant to find the partially melted candy was yellow, and eagerly popped it in her mouth, pocket lint and all. A sweet portent of a great day. Then, Betty recalled its origin. Last night, when leaving, she had brazenly scooped a small hand-full of candy out of the cashier Muriel's cache behind her cash register.

How could that snotty, flat chested witch keep a candy dish in front of her and still have some left at closing really bugged Betty almost as much as the cashier's reluctance to always ask credit card customers whether they wanted to include a tip with the charge. Yet, that same old biddy wanted a spiff from all the girl's tips. At times, life just seemed so unfair and definitely anti-bachelorette.

Walking five blocks from the downtown bus stop to Doctor Mellor's office, expended, at least, the caloric content of the small Hershey Bar with almonds waiting in Betty's purse. As long as she could hold her weight, chocolate would not hurt her or ever control her life again. Over indulgence and the resultant zits had made her teens miserable, but she had suffered no scarring and passing young men she met in the streets seemed to show interest, seemingly unaware of their age difference, or even more exciting, not caring.

Bouncing up three flights of stairs and consuming extra calories, Betty qualified for a full lunch, with triple chocolate dessert, if Doctor Mellor's scale confirmed her scale's reading. The manager and servers at Freddy"s would probably think her vain choosing to lunch there. Well, she was but also reluctant to be too dependent on a first time date, should things go wrong. She was proud that Tom had pursued her instead of younger waitresses.

Was Tom wholesome as he seemed, or had she been fooled again. Tom must have been married before or still, as he seemed masculine and choice. After two failed marriages, she knew how first impressions should not be trusted. Then too, had she projected her true self or was Tom reading her as an aging bunny needing conquest. Time would tell, and Betty reasoned that she had a lot of idle time to spare, and hopefully, share with someone appreciative.

In Mellor's office, she remembered her visit last week, when Doctor Mellor, who was always blase when with his patients, had seemed concerned, thoroughly palpating both breasts, under the paper gown, a frown furrowing his brow. "I guess we better get a little nip from this one here. We can do it here and know for certain that its just one of those harmless cysts that---You can come back next Tuesday, can't you? I'll have a report by then."

Tuesday was a late start day so it fit her schedule. As Betty sat on the worn and uncomfortable fake leather settee, a little fear penetrated the defensive shell she used to insulate herself from disappointments or rejections. The lobby was not crowded, probably because Dr. Mellor's practice was deteriorating. No woman likes to entrust her feminine mystique to someone who could desert her by dying. There was no other legitimate reason a woman would seek a younger Gynecologist, and Doctor Mellor's fees had not kept pace with or exceeded inflation. Medical insurance coverage was not included in tip income.

Halfway through a dog-aired Scientific American article on Peacocks, Betty discovered what happens to male peacocks when their gaudy tail feathers are removed, or even damaged. "Shamed and impotent, driven to solitude? Oh crap. Males are doomed by their silly egos," she told the far-away author. Tired of reading about human frailty, she closed her eyes.

Just short of napping, she was called and escorted was escorted to one of the examination rooms. Doctor Mellors came in before she had settled or even looked for another, more current magazine. He seemed crabby, unlike his usual mellow manner and gruffly began, "We waited too long, Betty. That little lump is not a cyst. It is a malignant and well-developed tumor. We've got to react quickly."

Betty assumed he was harsh to mask his pity, but was not going to let him off so easily. "What do you mean, we Doctor? Are we going to remove something of yours? Or are you planning to suggest a mastectomy and radiation? Are you assuming I want to live longer by letting someone butcher my body and leave me to scrunch scarred and deformed into a prosthetic brassiere that I would have to leave on even when making love? For fair consideration, how quickly would I be gone, if I did nothing but enjoy every last day I have?""Now Betty, don't overreact!" Frowning more than she had ever seen before, Doctor Mellors said, "There's nothing to suggest that tumor, however dangerous, did metastasize. If it has, even the tiniest bit, this could be your last Christmas . . . if we do nothing."

Not knowing where the impertinent words came from, she heard herself say, "Well, Screw you, Doctor. If WE die, WE die complete."

She realized she was walking out without paying or setting another appointment, and was in the lobby before she thought of apologizing. Yet, sweet old Doctor was not "We", even when trying to save or extend her life. Maybe tomorrow, she would take off from the job that she was soon destined to lose, and apologize, maybe submit to broadening her options.

Now, she had but one thought, and resolutely stomped the marbled length of the Medical Arts lobby, to the blind concessionaire's counter. It was a lustful spot smelling of warm chocolate Betty forced herself to ignore, each time she came in the building. She rapped on the top of the glass counter for the blind vendor's attention and roared, "Is that all the chocolate kisses you've got? I want them all!"

Betty breathed deeply, a sigh of relief. For the first time in forty-two years, she could pig-out on chocolate, without fear of acne or gaining weight. What wonderful way to die.

SO TRY AGAIN

God grew us in a moving sea
to know that tides return.
Tossed around by waves, a truth we see,
and one great lesson learn.

Twas not by one great crushing blow,
did sea it's triumph reach.
Insistent waves, both sure and slow,
turned rock to sandy beach.

So purposeful, recurring swells,
push back confining shore.
The sermon that the ocean tells
Is louder than its roar.

All obstacles that loom forlorn
might say you have to quit.

Persist like waves, surrender scorn,
because you won't submit.

JAIL THE GUN

On the third Thursday of each month, our Mystery Writer's Club devotes discussion time to diagraming plot development. The members describe their latest project to our group for constructive criticism. We don't have a written procedure, relying instead on common courtesy and tenure. This past Thursday, I felt entitled to be first presenter, being the only member with hise presentation ready who did not get a turn at last month's meeting.

My assumed right was usurped by a brazen new member who is our first novice since Bernard Smith, our current club president joined us. I was the one who brought in Bernie three years ago, so he should have protected my interest. Yet, this brash newcomer barged forward and appropriated my presentation time.

Whoever told him about our little group and its meeting schedule must have been somewhat ambivalent about recommending him, forcing him to present himself. That fact and the crass manner of his self introduction, had already convinced me, he was pushy and explained why he did not show deference to long time members.

This crass interloper, Fred Hopkins, was a tall slender man, slightly stooped, almost like a predatory crouch. If I were characterizing him in a story, I'd call him Mr. Pounce, and change his hair from his common sienna, to a greased, black pompadour, then portray him with a sinister moustache and shifty eyes. I certainly would not buy a used car from him, based on appearance alone. Some desperate women would consider him attractive, despite his steel grey eyes and cold stare. To me, he looked malevolent and opportunistic.

During his adulatory self-inauguration, Fred described himself as gregarious, but I saw him as audacious or even impertinent. Fred told us much more than we needed or ever wanted to know about his philosophy of life, genetic and geographical heritage, educational and employment background, travel and adventure experiences and even hinting at several outrageous sexual escapades. Finally, he launched into a convoluted and self-exalting presentation of his plot.

Hopkins had not called for the usual suggestions or criticism. With false modesty, he asked if anyone wanted to hear his plot for a perfect murder with the perpetrator immune from discovery or prosecution. I silently seethed while almost everyone clapped and he continued detailing his bizarre plot. While supposedly soliciting approval, Fred brazenly told us that our reactions didn"t matter as this was already a completed plot, impossible to change or revise. Since Fred did not call for our advice or involvement, why should we even participate. Yet, all of the members avidly listened to his malevolent story outline.

Not me. I was busy taking notes, preparing to challenge both his logic and characterization as totally implausible. I must admit, he was a good story teller, whether he could write or not. There were only two main characters and he defined them both as neither villain or hero. The murderer, incongruously cast as a busy tax accountant, secretly despised his victim and plotted his death with great deliberation. The motive for murder was weak and I can't recall how or why the victim provoked the murder. Yet I do remember every word of Fred's almost lyrical depiction of his killer's emotions. Fred made me feel I was a participant and I envied his gory adjectives.

As soon as he finished and asked if there were questions, I jumped to my feet, forgetting my notes, and they were unnecessary with all the improbabilities. I politely began, "Interesting story line, Fred, but why do you have Miller, the Accountant want to kill his kind and inoffensive neighbor? Mystery stories can't be based on chance or senseless killings, can they?"

Fred looked me straight in the eye and said, "Good question. I was focused on murder without consequences, not why it was committed. My plot is about how an obvious murderer escapes punishment by good planning. The story's raison d'etre is how it was accomplished. Tom Miller is an accountant only because that is my own background and expertise, which helped me to know him and his mental capacity. I still don't understand his hate for his neighbor or want to rationalize or even quantify that malice. Hatred is a human characteristic resident in varying degrees in all of us. Each one of us here will sometime have to sublimate evil intentions toward a person fate or circumstance forces you to tolerate. Forced amity breeds hate, just like the cleverly submerged hate everyone feels for his boss."

I pounced on his logic, politely asking, "You have Miller, plotting the murder using a weapon familiar only to his neighbor, Al Herbert. Herbert is the gun enthusiast and expert collector, yet your Miller uses a rather esoteric, if believable anomaly of one specific and very rare gun. Your whole plot is based on that idiosyncrasy, and you even have Herbert holding the gun.. Yet, Miller supposedly this entire scenario to be the victim's doing.. Doesn't this strain credulity?"

"Absolutely, and that is proof of Miller's genius. Miller had ingratiated himself with Herbert, embracing his neighbor's strong interest in antique guns. With good listening skills, Miller discovered the means to use one peculiar item in Herbert's prized gun collection as the murder weapon. What's more, he had the audacity and intellect to have the victim pull the trigger. In most states, they hang the shooter, not the target or victim."

I challenged again, "Why would Miller risk failure using an unfamiliar weapon, while trying to commit a perfect crime? Who should believe the murderer would use a weapon as incriminating as something unique to his victim's milieu?"

"If you ever commit murder, my friend, don't use an obvious weapon of your own trade or familiarity. The police would have had no reason to think Fred Miller, a naive accountant was an expert in old guns. Miller stealthily became one with Herbert amicably supplying that knowledge. Maliciously, Miller utilized his adversary's strength, as in Jiu Jitsu."

"Still don't seem logical to me that Miller could count on Herbert trying to shoot him with a booby-trapped gun."

"Miller didn't want to use a logical plan. He was only concerned with getting away with murder by baffling the authorities. The Justice System is very, very good at understanding logical murder plots."

Bernie, our moderator finally realized the merit of my challenges to Hopkin's logic, and also protested, "What was so strange about Miller's gun and key to the murder plot?"

Fred began his long and far-fetched explanation, "The Dilgas shotgun is a rare and expensive sporting weapon hand-made by Alphonso Dilgas, armorer for Spain's King in the sixteenth century. Dilgas made his famous gun by wrapping three half inch wide straps of high carbon Damascus steel around a twelve gauge mandrel of bronze and hammer welding them into a seamless gun barrel. Those barrels were stronger than anything made at that time and Dilgas owners valued these hand-crafted guns more than their mistress or their best hunting dog. The shot pattern of these guns was accurate and always consistent. Only a rare few of their owners knew their one weakness, which Herbert surreptitiously discovered.

The Dilgas shotgun had a lethal tendency for spiraled straps to unravel backward if the barrel became slightly plugged. Modern high velocity shells coupled with blockage, such as caused by the snug insertion of an object no more durable than a pickle or a tender young carrot, would cause violent explosion and backward unraveling of the plugged barrel. Miller chose to use his index finger. He told the investigators that sticking his finger in

Herbert"s gun was an unintended defensive reflex. Police find gun victims also have wounds to the hand from that same impulse and nodded affirmatively."

"Are you asking us to believe your murderer could deliberately plan and arrange such a mishap," I asked, "Have the confidence to goad his victim into pointing a loaded shotgun at him yet manage to jam his finger in the barrel then provoke the victim to pull the trigger, trusting the plugged barrel would rupture?"

"The authorities shared your disbelief that such a scheme could work. That was the whole intent of this plot. Be unbelievable. The obvious is easy to orchestrate but the incomprehensible takes much longer. You have an advantage over the prosecution as I will tell you that Miller's finger was already inserted in the Dilgas' gun barrel before he uttered the words that convinced Herbert to pull the trigger.

Curious myself, I asked, "Well, if he were close enough to the gun to plug the barrel with his finger, why was Miller not killed by the explosion and barrel unraveling? How could Miller situate himself to put his finger in the gun?"

"How difficult do you think it was to arrange a situation where Herbert finds his neighbor and supposed friend ominously holding his prized shotgun pointed at him while swearing his intent to shoot. Betrayed and desperate, Herbert tried to wrest away the gun, unaware that was an intricate part of Miller's plan. When Herbert easily gained partial control of the gun, he instinctively tried to fire even though he didn't know if it was loaded, what kind of shell it held, or that Miller"s finger was unobtrusively plugging the barrel."

Frustrated by his quick rationalization of the flaws in his logic, I persisted, "I cannot believe anyone would trust their life to the possibility that their finger in a gun barrel would cause a loaded gun pointed at them to explode, killing only the shooter."

"Oh Yes, it works. I swear on a stack of bibles, the shooter is dead", Fred said circling his right hand over an imaginary bible held in his left. "Who could prove that the intended victim set up the shooter's murder?"

All of us stared at his animated gesticulations, and some of us noticed that Fred"s right hand was terribly malformed and almost all of his right index finger was missing.

HOLSUM'S DILEMMA

Allen Holsum, is a man without fault, destined since birth to determine the flaws in all others, and decide the fate of those unfortunate citizens less perfect, who are brought to his courtroom. Elected Judge after only six years of law practice, he has occupied the bench exactly ten years and has yet to make any mistake. No one would consider him too lenient after studying his sentencing record yet, Judge Holsum often boasts that none of his rulings has ever been reversed.

On this uncelebrated anniversary, he is sure his judicial decision will be the right one, as always. For the first time in his tenure as Eden County Criminal Court Judge, he does not know how he will rule, and the prosecution had already rested. Not because he was inattentive for he heard, without being unduly influenced by supposed mitigating circumstances dug up by defense, nor did he doubt the guilt of the man standing before him. Unfortunately, clumsy prosecution had not provided legal basis to convict this brazen and obvious murderer. The prosecutor had failed and Judge Holsum felt obligated to impose justice.

Josiah Thorton candidly admitted facts that seemed to prove his intent to cause the death of his feared antagonist, Mr. McCaulley. The prosecutor's righteous indignation and lucid cross examination would have convinced almost all juries that Holsum had plotted and arranged the destruction of his enemy. Thorton had unwaveringly asserted his innocence, acting as his own defense attorney, and the prosecutor had not effectively countered his arguments of innocence. Quite tall and with ram-rod posture, Josiah looked upright. Clear blue eyes under an unruly thatch of straw colored hair gave Josiah a look of innocence contrary to facts.

Judge Holsum presumed more skillful questioning of Thorton would provoke admission of an indictable violation of Montana law and began his own, unusual interrogation carefully. "You have not presented much defense, Mr. Thorton. Before deciding on your guilt, I would like to summarize what has been revealed, thus far. Will that be acceptable?"

Josiah Thorton, beaming agreeably, nodded enthusiastically, then more properly added, "Yes, Your Honor."

"So, Mr. Thorton, Did you have any reason to hate the deceased Mr. McCaulley?"

"Well, he was a mean, wicked man, focused on ruining me, anyway that he could. Death would end that harassment. McCaulley told several people that he would destroy me and my honeybee rental business."

"Did you want him dead, Mr. Thorton?" Judge Holsum asked, gauging Josiah's reaction and noting a smirk of satisfaction betray Thorton's impassive mien.

"Everyone who knew him wanted him gone, one way or another," Thorton said. "I knew him better than some but not as well as others. All the apiarists in Eden County feared and hated him. He wanted all of the hive rental contracts with the hay growers, and would do anything to get them".

Holsum's clerk, who was the son of one of the large hay producers, had confirmed how zealously McCauley marketed the placement of his bee hives. The red clover growers so prevalent in Eden Valley were crucially dependent on bee pollination for success. Edward McCaulley was not popular among the dozen beekeepers in the Clover Springs Valley, and perhaps, with good reason. His court clerk also repeated the story of fierce competition between McCaulley and Thorton for a woman's love, who was now McCaulley's widow.

"Did you cause his death, Mr. Thorton?" the Judge said knowing full well that he had, but seeking something more indictable than evil wishes.

"McCaulley was stung by his own bees, Your Honor, and I was not acquainted with any of them, nor did I know how to instruct them, unless they could read my mind. I sure did not say, 'Sting your keeper', even if he did deserve it."

Judge Holsum, annoyed by Thorton's sarcastic reply, pointed his gavel at the self-confident defendant and demanded, "Do you know why his bees stung McCaulley, Mr. Thorton?"

"Maybe the bees knew him better than all of us in Clover Springs."

"I do not appreciate your sarcastic attempts at humor, Mr. Thorton. Your cause is best served with quick and truthful answers. Did Mr. McCaulley's own bees sting him because of the presence of Bee Moth larvae traces or residue on his person?"

"Bees are fiercely aggressive in defending their honey and pupae against Bee Moth, invasion. Bee Moths lay eggs that mature into larvae that gobble up the wax protecting honey bee larvae, and encasing the hives honey. I certainly would advise any beekeeper to never wear anything that smelled of Bee Moths, or their larvae."

"Mr. Thorton, Did you hear the prosecutor say that traces of pyralidae larvae were found on McCaulley? Isn't that the larvae of Honey Wasps?"

"Yes, your honor. More properly, Galleria Mellonella, which is of that family division, and is a deadly scourge of all apiarists."

"How did those larvae get on McCaulley? Mr. Thorton?"

"I honestly believe, it was self administered, although originally it was contaminating me." Josiah said, revealing a smile.

"Please explain, Mr. Thorton. Are you responsible in any way, for that larvae getting on McCaulley?"

"I think not. McCaulley himself is the one responsible. I had just cleaned a honey moth infected hive that had once been McCaulley's, and evidently had some larva traces on me when McCaulley threw me off his front porch. He might have picked up that dangerous contaminant on his hands while assaulting me, then wiped it on more parts of his body?"

"Isn't the usual practice of you bee keepers to carefully burn infected hives, Mr. Thorton?"

"That is usually, strongly recommended, but most bee

keepers are reluctant to destroy their bees. For instance, McCaulley has never destroyed a hive, but has sold many hives that were infected. Chris Larson, bought several of his infected hives, and complained to me. I felt sorry for him as a newcomer and decided to destroy the few larvae and Honey moth eggs in that hive. My duty as a Beekeepers Association officer was to inform McCaulley that he had sold an infected hive. It was his duty to repay the buyer and arrange for safe incineration of that hive. Not Mr. Larson, who trusted McCaulley and bought his first three hives from him, paying double the usual rate."

"Did you know how bees would react to that larva, Mr. Thorton," asked Judge Holsum?

"Just as they did, Your Honor. Bees and Bee keepers are deathly afraid of Honey Moths," Thorton said, wrinkling his brow in feigned concern.

"Did you know that both you and Mr. McCaulley could be now fatally attacked if you came near a hive?" the Judge asked, peering intently into the eyes of Thorton.

"Yes, I worried about being stung, myself." Josiah paused, then thought of adversary's fate, reportedly stung over three thousand times by the vigilante bees, and possibly felt some degree of sympathy. Thorton really felt more sympathy for the three thousand bees who had given their lives in the kamikaze attack on something smelling of Honey Moth. Painful death for both, he imagined.

"So what did you do to prevent being stung, Mr. Thorton?" Judge Holsum surveyed Josiah"s eyes, detecting as usual, no hint of deceit in his answers.

"I took a shower soon as I got home. Even before I treated the scrapes and bruises from McCaulley's fists."

"Mr. Thorton. did you ever tell Edwin McCaulley he might be contaminated with Honey Moth Larvae, knowing that you and your clothing were full of their crushed remains from cleaning the Moth infected hive?"

"Well, I didn"t tell him he was or wasn't. It was originally his hive, and he was responsible. McCaulley was only concerned with hurting and embarrassing me, and wouldn't have listened to me, anyway. He should have taken a shower before visiting his bees, but he often neglected to take a shower. Many people have told me that McCaulley stunk. If the bees could talk, they would probably say they stung McCaulley just because he stunk."

"Why would McCaulley visit his bees, right after you left him, Mr. Thorton?" Truthfully answered, this could prove Thorton"s complicity, the Judge rightfully calculated.

"He knew I was right with my accusation and was probably concerned that more of his hives were infested. Maybe someone called and told him that some of his hives had been tipped over. He probably thought that I had, since I had also accused him of tipping over my hives. He did, I didn't. Whoever tipped over his hives and whoever called McCaulley caused his death, not me!"

"Didn't you, in fact tip, over his hives while you were angry from the fracas on the porch? You drove right by the hives when you left, and were angered and humiliated. Isn't that right, Mr. Thorton?"

"No, Your Honor! That would've have been good reason to rightfully charge me with his murder. If I had gone near his hives or any others, I would have also been fatally stung, too. You should know that I am only guilty of fearing my oppressor. How can you consider me guilty of his murder? If I were guilty, I would have hired a lawyer, instead of defending myself."

"You have admitted that you did provide one of the causative factors in Mr. McCaulley's death, and you certainly have not expressed remorse, or even denied murderous intent."

"I will not say I regret that Mr. McCaulley will no longer harass me and his other victims including his wife, for that would be untruthful. I have answered all questions concerning Mr. McCaulley's death, honestly."

"Your candidness has impressed me, Mr. Thorton. If that

also means, truthfully, do you agree that you are half guilty?"

"Yes, your honor, but only if that signifies, I am half innocent," challenged Thorton.

"Because the state has not brought forward an accomplice, I regretfully find you not guilty. Too bad that the prosecution did not choose to charge you with planned carelessness. You are free to go. If anymore of your enemies die of similar suspicious circumstances, I hope you will choose a jury trial, not a trial by a Judge dedicated to upholding the letter of the law, and whose decisions have never been reversed!"

WHEN

Don't cry my child, Here!, dry your eye,
*   our King will build so we can't die,*
*   a Space-War shield called SDI,*
*   when Eagles swim and Codfish fly!*

The sick and old we'll hide no more,
*   we'll scrap our guns to feed the poor,*
*   love humanity and Peace restore*
*   when Lions sing and Robins roar!*

Past enemies, their friendship spurn.
*   We build more bombs to sadly learn,*
*   that it's not Peace those weapons earn,*
*   when mountains melt and rivers burn!*

LOVER'S LIES

Accelerating slowly to fifty while still in the safety lane, Bill carefully checked in his left rear mirror for a proper break in the now alerted and suddenly legal traffic lane. All oncoming drivers nervously surveyed the roadside where a New Jersey Highway Patrolman had just given him a speeding ticket but had not yet moved nor doused his flashing blue light.

Bill knew he should have fully turned his head if he were now driving in the exemplary manner that he had just spent twenty minutes describing, but his neck was stiff from tension induced by this disastrous interruption in his hectic weekend schedule. After explaining the seriousness of his mission and the forgivable reason for haste, he had expected a warning ticket. Officer Johnson, most certainly Swedish, tall and blonde, with pale blue eyes, seemed so trusting and gullible. Otherwise, Bill would not have tried the "First ticket in years," gambit which, when checked and proven untrue, probably negated all chances for a warning ticket.

He would not he have tried, "Just moving with the rest of the traffic," if he known Officer Johnson had been following closely a long time and saw him weave through the jerks obstructing good traffic flow. Because he spent so much time pleading, first for exoneration, then mercy.
He could just barely catch his flight out of Newark.

He would not be able to swing by his new girl friend's condo in South Orange, expecting her to take a cab. They were a thing from the first day Nancy Schiller came to work as the new receptionist. Not continuously, as Nancy ended their surreptitious romance, three times in the next two months. Bill was a good salesman before his promotion to the home office as Dealer Network Manager, and used those persuasive skills to re-kindle the illicit affair, each time it fizzled.

By now, Nancy had learned almost all of the flaws in her lover and adjusted her expectations, becoming resigned to her tenuous love life. Confidently, Bill extracted his phone from the brief case in the back seat and activated the number three redial button. Nancy answered before the second ring. Hell, she probably was holding the phone and already mad.

"Grab a cab, Honey", he began slowly, preoccupied with groping for the best reason for missing her pickup, then more quickly, and with confidence, "Traffic was bad all the way down and I had to take the ditch to avoid a rolled semi. I stopped to pull the driver out and had just finished treating him for shock, when the Patrolman arrived. He held me over an hour while he filed the accident report. I was in a dead spot, couldn't even get your phone to ring!"

Nancy's usual huskily sexy voice screeched irritatingly higher and tense, as she challenged, "Why didn't you spend the night with me like we planned. You were with your family down at the shore again, weren't you? I think I'll stay home. I knew, when I called your place last night, that you had call forwarding switched to your mobile phone. I can tell the difference in the ring, so I called back after you shut it off and the operator said..."

"Nancy. Don't be paranoid, you've got it all wrong!" and thinking quickly, responded with the sure-fire placation. "I was a bit devious last night, because I wanted to surprise you. I met with my lawyer and we beered up too much for me to drive home. I stayed at the Holiday, reluctant to drive" he said while while his mind searchef for a good story.

Maybe their relationship should end, and truthfully relaying how he spent last night could start that break-up ugliness. But not this weekend. He had told two of the more skeptical salesman that he was bringing his new girlfriend to the meeting, and needed Nancy's presence as proof. Already skeptical, they looked for flaws in his tales of salacious adventures. Bill was prone to continue embellishment of exposed and obvious falsehoods.

Last week, one new salesman had disparagingly called him Pinocchio and emulated the grasping a growing nose with his upraised fist. Having Nancy there with him in Vegas, would shock them and maybe corroborate some of his exaggerated and previously challenged exploits. Bill wanted Nancy with him, but only peripherally as top management thought family men were more dependable when they promoted. Jack would have to do some fancy talking to adroitly manage both proving and hiding his secretary's dual role.

Breathing deeply, he began again, "My lawyer came up with a great game plan, on how I can retain most of my assets, for us, Honey. I hate being devious, and would prefer to just tell my old battleaxe that it's all over, but that would leave us with damned little of what I've worked so hard for. Let's follow a careful game plan, even if it delays getting together."

"B.S., Jack!" She said explosively, reminding Jack he had told Nancy that his lawyer was on Army Reserve duty when she had asked why he hadn't came up with something. "You just can't tell the same story twice, and the whole office knows it! You promised to let Granger know about us on this trip. You think you can keep our relationship from the boss, while I act like I came along to...Ah, that's it. You want me to miss the plane because you've got cold feet!"

"Aw come on, Nancy, work with me on this. Grab a cab. I arranged to sit with old man Granger on the way out, just to tell him about us." Now how the hell was he going to arrange that, he thought as he spoke. Mr. Granger was sitting in first class. Maybe it was best if Nancy didn't come. Only that lecherous accountant Ed Bailey, with his relentless search for expense account improprieties had discovered he and Nancy were a number. Ed checked the address that the flowers Jack reported sending to his Topeka distributor's sick wife, was really to Nancy. Jack had blithely covered Ed's challenge until the accountant asked, "Do you send allyour customer's wives flowers inscribed, 'With all my love!" Now he would have to be more innovative on his expense account since Baily would be on guard.

"You haven't told your wife or your boss about getting a divorce, have you Jack? You are going to make me a complete fool, aren't you?" Nancy waited for an answer and the seconds tolled by.....

Well he wouldn't be sitting in first class, so he needed a quick story, to cover his rash claim. "Yes, I forgot. I did give up my seat with Granger so I could switch with who sits with you."

"How in Hell will you sit with me, dummy. I can"t get to the airport by cab in time. You don't dare sit with me. You want me to get stranded trying, as you don't have the guts to tell me that you don't want me there!"

There was his chance! Jack tried to tell the truth but reverted to character, explaining slowly like to a child. "I'll simply catch Granger on the golf course, I'll be in his foursome, he said. I'll tell him we are getting married as my wife is leaving me. He will support me when I explain that it is all her choice."

"Jack, you told me you had not divorced Bertha sooner because she was Granger"s second cousin. You can't remember your lies, and yet you expect me to believe them. Just once, give me the truth. Why did you ask me to come to a convention I wasn"t a part of?"

When he and Nancy first started dating, she was so trusting that he had not remembered every detail on the complex explanations for his marital status and frequent inabilities to fulfill his suitor's objections. Now, she challenged everything he said, ending their relationship just when he was most interested in sustaining it. Nancy, pretty and twenty years younger than Bill, was great for his ego but he had mixed feelings about having a secret relationship which did nothing to depict his still functional sex appeal.

Thinking desperately aware the long silences following her questions was increasing Nancy"s suspicion, he resumed, "Nancy, wait something's wrong..." and something turned very wrong in his chest before he finished saying, "With my car." Clutching his chest with one hand, tried but failed to negotiate a safe stop on the shoulder. Doubling over in pain, he felt the car turning more to the left and tilting as it plunged through the small trees and ornamental shrubbery isolating the freeway from the adjoining countryside.

The car stopped, wedged between two trees, hidden from the highway. "Nancy, Nancy, call 911, have them find me... six miles past... 39 turn off. I'm having a heart attack. Quick...please, Nancy. I don't want to..." The phone slipped from his fingers.

"Yeah sure, I wondered what you'd come up with next, Pinnochio," and Nancy slammed down the receiver.

THE DRUMS OF WAR
No more War, the Maiden cried.
Brave new soldiers she would ignore
and pray they all, with love denied,
would shed the urge to march to war.
Die for Peace, the Kings decide.
We must choose priests, Sovereigns adore.
and seek to bless our countryside
with dead men downed on distant shore.
Another war! Sad parents cried.
When War Gods call for sons once more.
we'll just raise girls, true gender hide
for it's just men who march to war.
Dead for Peace and earthworms glide
through flesh turned loam, from grisly gore,
but leave eye sockets opened wide
to tearless stare for evermore.

LIFETIME OF LOVE

Jodie turned quickly, looking behind him for the thing he knew watched him, or did he just feel foolish about practicing new coolness? Or was someone actually spying on him while he furtively tried flipping a cigarette into the air and miraculously snatching it between his teeth, like his older brother, Stan? No one there. Jodie knew about this feeling of awareness in books and now he could definitely feel an alien presence. His residence was screened from the street by a high privacy fence and his parents and older brother Stan, had not came home from work.

Jodie too, should have been at his job packing bags at Budgeteer Foods, but he had asked the Store Manager for permission to leave early to pick up his Graduation Suit. It already hung in his closet. Jody fished out another fresh and stiff cigarette from the pack he had borrowed from Stan's room and positioned it in his palm for another try at his older brother's adroit, girl-attracting shtick.

The alien presence he suspected, stuck a small elfin head above the patio fence and said, "If you're insistent on killing yourself, those cigarettes take too long, especially when they aren't lit." Presently, more of her and her shiny red running suit appeared above the fence, as if she were on a ladder. Very small and quite wrinkled, she seemed a cross between his younger grandmother and the gnome-like character pictured on the beer ad for Finian's Green Ale.

Before he gained composure enough to speak, she continued, "I'll show you how to do that trick, with a real neat twist." Then placing two small wrinkled hands on the top of the eight foot high redwood fence, she catapulted over, landing lightly on bright red Nikes, softly like a cat.

Awed, Jody blustered, "I could feel someone watching me. How long have you been spying on me?"

"Sometime shorter than when you were an evil grin in your Father's Eye and much longer than just now. I know you really well, Jody Brown!" Then she gave a big blink, or wink with both eyes, and sprawled out on the grass, like an elegant scarecrow, disentangled from its frame and draped at his feet.

Jody looked at the mystical creature, and liked her immediately even if she were the sixty years old, she looked, but how in Hades Hell had she scampered over the tall fence if she was that old. Something strange was happening. He had nothing better to do until his family came home for supper and the timer on the microwave holding TV Dinners already said the Brown family reconvened at five.

His curiosity, source of most Jody's embarrassments, compelled him to try again, "Who are you and why do know who I am? And how the heck did you fly over that fence?"

"Maybe I"m a monkey with a tail I tuck away in my pants, or just one fascinating old lady. Women over thirty, never tell their age. Boy, I have much to teach you. I am a woman of mystery and magic that no sweet young man like you could ever understand. I know all about you because you are the most handsome young man in Paradise Valley, maybe in the whole state of Georgia. Why shouldn't I want to know all about you?"

While Jody continued to stare open-mouthed and speechless at her strange appearance, he accepted her flamboyant flattery as fact. The strange intruder wore a strange little beret of red satin, matching the jump suit, which miraculously stayed fixed atop her burnished silver hair, despite her animated movements. He marveled at her brazen confidence, suspecting that she was unlike anyone he had ever met before. Should he ask for three wishes, he wondered.

The visitor quickly rolled back into a supine crouch, then sprung to her feet, like a jumping jack. Jody's chin dropped farther and he could feel his breath whistling into his gaping mouth.

"Here, let me show you how to do that cigarette trick, you"ve been trying all week," as she deftly extracted Stan"s cigarette package from Jody"s back pocket of his tight jeans, quicker and slicker than any pickpocket. Then, pulling out one crumpled poisonous coffin nail, she stiffened it between her left forefinger and thumb, then dropped it carefully into that quickly opened palm. Quickly, she flipped it skyward, while staring straight ahead at Jody's wide open eyes. At the last fraction of a second, she tipped her head back to catch that cigarette between her teeth, and it was lit and trailing smoke.

     "My God", he said incredulously, "How do you do that?"

     "No way, your God, Sweety. Maybe I'm your good fairy. I haven't decided yet. Here Sweety," she said before kissing him quickly, but more powerfully than he had ever been kissed before. Jody blushed, embarrassed but envious of her self confident and brash demeanor. "Go put on your shorts and best running shoes and run with me.   If you can catch me, I"ll give you the other half of that kiss and I'll show you how to do that trick and some tricks even more amazing."

     Slightly regaining his composure and youthful confidence, Jody rashly replied. "Don"t need anything special to keep up with you. I could catch you if I want to, and I already know that cigarette trick is impossible. I must have been hypnotized." He imagined the startled audience, if the little old sprite could truly empower him with her magic. Prudently spurning the aerial route over the fence, he went to the gate by the garage and opened it while his strange antagonist zipped through, getting a head start of at least two seconds, while he stood flat-footed, wondering if the strange creature was real, or an apparition, like her lighted cigarette.

     "Catch me if you can, little man," she hollered back in a cracked shriek, something like Dorothy's wicked witch, and sailed down Morgan lane toward Hartzell Creek and its long parkway.

     She must be real, he realized as he could still taste something lingering on his lips from her kiss. A bit like the sweet but chemical taste of the pills his Cross Country Track Coach dispensed before meets. He set out toward the familiar parkway, where he often trained. Jody"s prime cross country running asset was endurance, not speed, so he loped after her confident that he would eventually catch her. "Then, what will I do", he asked himself, uncertain but eager to find out.

After running several miles, trailing always just a few feet behind, no matter how hard he pressed, the sprite-like old dame slowed, leaving the pathway, heading uphill toward a large cluster of Purple Crepe Myrtle bushes. Jody did not remember seeing that large copse of flowers before, but followed as his nemesis ran knowingly into the planting. There was a grassy clearing inside where the dizzying fragrance seemed to converge. The miraculous old magician allowed his outstretched arms to encircle her in a tumbling tackle.

"You've caught Felicia. You have won yourself a whole lifetime of love and riches," she said without the slightest hint of labored breathing from the run. Felicia turned her head almost directly toward him, though the rest of her body was pinned, facing the ground. As she smiled, many of her facial wrinkles pulled tight and virtually disappeared. Somehow, the rest of her body, turned too, matching her head, facing him. Jody realized that she had been eautiful, but that was history.

A Silent minute passed before Jody remembered the words in her original challenge. Pinning her hands, Jody realized it was because Felicia allowed it. "Now, how do I do that impossible trick?" He demanded.

"Nothing is impossible. Some things just haven't been done yet. I will teach you how to do many impossible things, but first, a kiss." Felicia easily slid loose both hands and pulled him down into an embrace, before he could speak. That kiss made Jody shiver while generating cold sweat on his face. It was not at all like kissing either of his grandmothers. Intrigued and enchanted, he discovered lust that he was embarrassed to show or even know.

Felicia eagerly felt his lust, and whispered in his ear, "I know how hard you"ve tried, but you have not yet made love to any one. It is now the right time."

Jody could not speak, but shook his head negatively, admitting what he would never tell anyone. At Seventeen, he had tried often, but was always so clumsy and dorky, that all attempts had failed, even with girls reputed generous and wordly.

Felicia took complete charge while Jody, numbed by shock, remained silent but eagerly compliant. Her kisses seem to pull his insides out, her hands were electric. Lying spent and exhausted Jody, breathed deeply hoping to regain his breath. Felicia, showing no evidence of their exertion, took off his shoes. She began to forcefully massage his feet sending surprising electric shocks to far distant and seemingly connected parts of his body.

Felicia broke the electric silence, saying breathlessly, "Now this is the most important thing I will teach you. That is how to give love to someone."

Jody could not speak or protest. Paralyzed, afraid that saying anything would interrupt her actions, Jody closed his eyes and shivered with pleasure. As if anything could deter or distract his whirlwind attacker

Felicia spoke again, "Foot rubs, kind words, special kisses, snuggling and hugs are empty physical tokens unless one gives much more than they expect in return."

After a gloried two hours, that seem an eternity, a satiated Felicia, allowed Jody freedom to talk, and catch his breath. Now aware of reality, Jody begged, "Let me up, Felicia. My folks will be looking for me."

"And now you want your magic trick? Don't look so abashed, Jody. Isn"t that why you tried so hard to please me?"

Jody ill at ease, stammered clumsily, "Why, no, I ah guess. Yah but uhh....."

"Well, you now have that magical power, but there is a frightful price to pay. If you EVER do that one impossible trick, I am gone from your life forever." Felicia waved a milk white, wrinkle-free hand with a flourish worthy of the most flamboyant stage magician, and presto, the hand held a cigarette. She extended the white tube toward Jody, and asked. "Do you want to see me disappear? Do you want to never see me again?"

Jody stood transfixed. Somehow Felicia looked much younger and prettier. She had taught him other more wonderful tricks that he liked better than magical cigarettes. He threw the cigarette to the ground and squashed it with his foot, as if it were a cockroach, although he had suspicion that he had been flimflammed. "Can't I do the trick just once, to see that I can?"

"Not if you you would like to spend more time with me. I can arrange to have you drive me all around the country in a new Stingray? Show you delightful places and pleasures. We would spend the summer, seeing the USA in a hot new Chevrolet? You can drive, can't you? I can come by your house, later tonight, and make it happen."

Perplexed, Jody turned away. Picturing lusty Felicia confronting his stern and conservative father then blushed as he pictured his mother's shock at the implications. He laughed with disbelief, heartily, barely able to answer. "Sure you can, but wait until I'm upstairs in bed. I'll turn in early because tomorrow, I graduate. I don't want to watch my parents explode."

"Go home now, my sweet young Marco Polo. There is so much of the World you have to see and taste," Felicia said, pointing east, as though, to a wayward puppy. Jody, set off running for home, while sure that he had experienced magic he would never know again.

Providentially, everyone at home was running late. They were just seating at the table. Jody was sure that his past activities had indelibly stained his face and body with the marks of sin. Exultant yet with his awakening, he was sure it showed for all to see. His mother was pleasant, as always, inquiring, "Did you have a good day, dear. Last day of classes, right? Are you ready to face the world?"

His Dad, breaking rules, was sneaking a look at the Evening Telegram, but looked up to add, "Will you work work at

Budgeteer this summer? Did they offer you a full-time job?

Stan chimed in, "I can get you on the night shift relief crew at the plant, if you want some real muscle building work, Jody."

Jody, voraciously hungry, addressed them all. "I Don't know what I will do, yet. I want something meaningful, that pays more than the Budgeteer."

Stan, rarely treated Jody as an adult, but conferred first recognition of Jody's maturation, "Wanna go shoot some pool at Eddy's? The Plant Super, hangs in there Thursdays. He'd hire you, I'm sure."

"Hey thanks, Stan! I got things happening. I'll find something, Saturday. Tonight, I"m going to catch up on my sleep. I'm hitting the bed, soon as I fill my face."

Seeing his mother in shock at his declaration of early bedtime, he tried disarming compliments, "Grrrreat! Mom's famous meat loaf special. Awesome, I'm really starved."

In the morning, he overslept. His mother, sat at the kitchen counter, slowly sipping her coffee. She paused, then asked. "Why didn't you tell us about your heroic life-saving adventure and the great summer joboffer? Am I ever jealous. I think working for Felicia Lawless would be a truly great learning experience."

Jody reeled in shock! Felicia had not been joking. While he slept, Felicia came by and by and talked to his parents. He could not imagine what she could have said or life-saving. Or how she could word a proposition of employment as innocent or worthy of his parents blessing. He listened in amazement as his mother recounted, first a call from a Mrs. Felicia Lawless, who told how Jody had heroically acted to save an old woman's life and earned her gratitude. She, being sinfully rich and eager to travel, wanted to reward Jody with a job, all summer, as her chauffeur. She would endow his first year's tuition and provide all board and keep, as well. She also would furnish all of his spending money while they traveled. Felicia had 'snowed' his parents.

She needed Jody to drive because she had never learned to

steer any thing but horses, and had ordered a sporty new Chevrolet Corvette for a summer-long, whirl-wind tour of the whole North American continent. Less than a week ago, Felicia's contracted driver had grown sick from a rare disease called Progeria. that causes premature aging and early death.

So very sad, for the 'old' driver, but a great opportunity for Jod y. He would have an adventure and learning experience while earning college tuition and lightening the financial burden of his parents. They exultantly agreed Jody should jump at the chance.

Stan, breakfasting too, obviously late for work, was even jealous of Jody's impending good fortune and joked that he should be paid in advance, considering his patron's maturity and questionable lifeline. For the first time in his life, Jody replied harshly to his brother and hero, "Your jealous, man. You don't know how to treat a dignified and classy lady," Saying more, he feared, would have him giggling from at his duplicity, and might reveal Felicia's real intentions..

Amazingly, Jody's summer of adventure and discovery began the morning after his graduation, which he had endured in a trance, apprehensively mesmerized by his encounter with Felicia. She came by in a taxi, and the impatient driver suffered, while Jody's mother nervously helped Jody pack. Felicia watched their effort, assuring both mother and son that whatever was forgotten would be easily purchased along the way. Jody marveled at his new benefactor's aplomb, no guilt on her impassive face. Jody tried to control a blush that rose to his face, eager to escape examination of his mother, who had always detected each sin, with a sixth sense which now seemed deactivated.

In the cab on the way to pick up their new car, Felicia said proudly, loud enough for the even the cab driver to hear, "Now, you are mine, baby." and embraced him lustily. Jody blushed, probably for the last time that summer.

After an indecent interval

The mismatched adventurers had returned to Atlanta after t Labor Day, whizzing magicallythrough the traffic jams. Felicia insisted touring bars before going to their motel. None considered Jody underage, but he was tired, and fearful of meeting local people who might recognize him. He surrendered, as usual. A few dances and few drinks, yet Jody awakened groggy. He struggled out of bed, joints stiff and sore and sadly noticed more hair lost to his crumpled and overworked pillow. Felicia snored, sleeping soundly, looking more beautiful than ever. Jody still puzzled why she detested and banned mirrors, while becoming so lovely. He Struggled shaving his tougher, more masculine beard by touch, as the bathrooms always had the mirror removed. Jody felt his face was wrinkling despite being seldom outside of bedrooms.

Jody knew his health had deteriorated during this summer's indulgences. Jody was sure hoped his vitality would return, once away from Felicia and her pleasurable but debilitating excesses. He now knew that there is risk in receiving too much of anything. With just a little will-power, he could end his summer of debauchery. He tapped his elegant silver electric razor to dislodge the fresh accumulation of stubble and numbly realized, most of it was gray. He stumbled shirtless to the outside door of their suite and strangely found it, uncharacteristically, unlocked. Out the door, and down the balcony steps, Jody scampered toward the corner gas station three blocks south. Groping in his pants pocket with his trembling right hand, Jody found the wad of bills, remaining from Felicia's daily dole, unspent the night before.

In the station, Jody separated a bill from his wad of money for the attendant and asked for a cigarettes. "Any brand, just give me a pack of smokes!"

Despite his minor age, the attendant did not doubt his legal age and threw him the most advertised and popular brand, asking, "Need matches?"

Wistfully, Jody answered, "I certainly hope not!" He ran to the station's bathroom, seeking privacy and tore open the pack, Jody pushed out a fresh cigarette, closed his eyes, then flipped it into the air, and without trying, felt it catch between his lips. Felicia had warned that doing the trick would send her away, and with great hope, he opened his eyes. Miraculously, the business end of his cigarette wafted smoke, signifying his liberation. Felicia warned she would be gone if ever he did the forbidden trick. Jody had survived a lifetime of love, spent during just one summer. He turned and for the first time since meeting Felicia, Jody saw a mirror. Last night while carousing, Jody worried that friends or family would see him with Felicia. Small chance. The face in the mirror was that of a very old man.

MEA CULPA

For fifty years, my needs came first.
The first wine poured assuaged my thirst,
but passing years, do grace incline
so first I pour my guest their wine
and patient wait until they taste
to see if it's with venom laced.
I once refused to share my food,
though no one thought me cheap or rude
since those who sniffed what I prepared
were thankful that it was not shared.
Real reason that my kitchen stunk
was dishes I'd forgot to dunk.
My life's been long, no sins I've claimed.
Of penal crimes, I won't be blamed.
No one will mourn when my life ends
I've chased away all trace of friends.
My written words that linger still,
present some worth, good purpose fill.
Hear me for this warning ample.
Don't be just negative example.

SIMON'S SECRET LIFE

Sandra Novotnik, stiffly straightened, after clumsily pulling herself out of her brother's low slung sport coupe, tugging with her strong left hand on the top of the unframed window glass. Sam, her visiting brother, sweetly allowed her the use of his new car, while he still slept, probably for the whole four hours of her split shift at Sheltered Arms. Use of his car seemed a feeble compensation for her hospitality, if she counted the fast depletion of her cupboard and liquor stock.

Bryan, the youngest of the ten Novotnik kids had been obnoxiously officious in describing how damaging and dangerous her manner of exiting cars was to her and his new "mystery" sports car. Although she was not psychic nor a believer in the occult, it seemed he was looking over her shoulder. The first time he let her drive his new toy, Bryan fussed over how suddenly she accelerated. She had been extra careful, seeing the same police car that had alarmed him. If the door glass did change alignment, she would insist that it was the result of sloppy British quality control.

"Ain't no way to get out of them foreign race cars, Sandy," came smugly from the towering old chevy station wagon, on her left, driven for the past twelve years by equally old and reliable George Smittern. George had been the night janitor and maintenance man at the nursing home, since it opened eight years ago, and he arrived and parked in the same stall ever since, except for one three day work suspension. That was while he was investigated for assaulting a wild and unruly patient, Simon Ware, who later confessed that his accusation was false. George was still sassy after his ten hour shift..

George was still stretched out rolling up the car window, giving her time to frame a suitable retort as she walked down the long lanai to the employee entrance. "If you old farts could park in the center of the stall, I'd have enough room to get out without doing a jig. I guess you've forgotten how to drive anything in right," which was an appropriate zinger, but not up to her usual

level. Sandy pulled open the door and shutting off any reply.
Sandra went immediately to her first charge, comatose and feeble;
Simon Ware was as ready as he would ever be.

*Straining with futility against his bonds for the hundredth
time, during the past night, Simon exercised again the resolve that
had allowed him to resist his tormentors. He had been
overwhelmed, not surrendered, and had giving his captors nothing
but his Army Serial number. Eyes closed, his Hadassah-trained
ears still recognized the approaching footsteps of the beautiful
White Russian Intelligence Chief who would make another attempt
at cracking his silence..*

   Laying her hand gently on his un-sleeved arm allowing
access to the semi-permanent needle block, Sandra tried to make
her presence known. She asked, "Are you awake, Mr. Ware?"
pitifully aware comatose Simon did not focus or move his eyes or
show any other sign of awareness.
   Mrs. Landing, Nursing Supervisor, stuck her head in,
apparently checking out her mysterious new nurse, covering the
intrusion with the polite comment, "I can't get over how you treat
the numb brains with more consideration than you do those
patients that bitch if they're offended. Ware's daughter is stopping
by, before lunch, so I guess, he does have relatives. Don't forget
the staff meeting at ten, Be nice to have all you aids there, all
caught up, for a change."
   As if to prove her point, Sandra began loosening Mr.
Ware's wrist restraints. Sandr thought it appropriate that patients
were untied, while bathed, whether they could benefit, or not. Mrs.
Currant in 309 had vacated the previous day, and though Pleasant
Arms had a long waiting list, another day empty for airing her
room. Sandra had a full complement of patients, but appreciated
new vacancies. With one less, her remaining patients would all
have a better care, and Sandra began bathing Simon Ware.

"So, finally giving up on torture, Aye," gloated Simon. Neither honey or stick would break Simon Ware though he would enjoy the vixe's blandishments as it had been such a long time. and with his bindings loosened, he was certain his skills as an oft-sought lover would numb his torturer enough for him to dive through the unbarred window. Simon worked at remembering his first and most bizarre sexual adventure to be ready for a extraordinary performance that would put his torturer in a trance long enough for him to hurl himself through the room's lightly meshed window and into the tree tops just barely visible. Yes, his trusty tool must not fail him and he thought of his governess with the fat fingers and her exploration while they both pretended he was napping....

Sandra well knew the procedure for bathing patients, but often indulged her speculative curiosity and ventured just a little into the patient's private area. That was fun especially when she initiated reactions that caused great embarrassment to her healthier male patients. Those carefully staged accidental caresses, which never seemed intentional, were an accumulated skill Sandra learned and could safely practice on comatose males. Never before had she achieved such grand results with someone as insensate as Simon Ware. Sandra conscientiously considered writing a report for the Day Superintendent, regarding her discovery of Simon's miraculous rejuvenation, long dead flesh coming to life.

Well aware of potential consequences, Sandra decided to let sleeping dogs lie or not to notice when they stood up, raring to go hunting. No one had questioned her references and she had left out all of the unpleasantness back in Beaver Falls. Any suspicions of patient abuse could lead to speculation or suspicions that might send someone digging unnecessarily through her work records, and go prying at her prior employers. Anyway, the honor of discovery should fall to 'Fatso Connie' who probably never provoked or saw erections on men dead or alive. Sandra knew the therapist was due to exercise and massage Simon's immobile limbs and she could hear the swok, swok, swok sound her thick legs made rubbing together as she came down the hall. Sandra ducked into the linen room, before Connie came around the corner, struggling to suppress snickers over the shock Connie would suffer. Later during her break in her shift, she would check with her brother, Sam. He would know whether Simon's improvement was a problem.

Simon felt a few rocks lift from the pile crushing his diaphragm, and inhaled enough to almost fill his brain with blood. More came loose and his sight returned, and though it was dark, he could see it was one the squaws who had buried him with rocks just a few hours ago. Full moon lit her face and he could see her eyes shining. It was the beautiful one who had so cruelly tortured and stripped away the yellow-striped pants that was the only remnant of his calvary uniform, but now she was removing the pile of stones that had been slowly suffocating him. The stones were gone, his hands and feet were still staked to the ground. The nubile young maiden was brushing away the stinging ants who were planning to carry him away, bite by bite. She was rubbing a soothing Indian balm over his abused and tormented body for some reason privy to her desires. Trapped and condemned to death, he was the last survivor of the Indians surprise attack. The Indian magic balm worked and he felt good. Very good. He puzzled why did she not release him and then discovered that he was now her captive and surrendered his last resistance.

Connie quickly cleaned up the tattle-tale mess, then spilled a camouflaging bit of the blue lotion on the stained spread, and began to wipe it up. The duty nurse could arrange the replacing of Simon's dislodged catheter as that was a procedure Connie was not licensed to do. Removal had been easy in spite of the inflated internal retainer bulb. My god, what had she done and where did she get the nerve. None of the patient's rooms had locks and people popped in often. Her real sin had been curiosity. She had been shocked and aroused by her first sight of a brightly lit, erect male penis. She had only tried to clinically examine that part of an almost corpse who would never tell or ever wake. No matter, as long as the aberrant organ was flaccid now

Connie decided to finish the scheduled massage, not out of gratitude, but guilt, and to explain the long time spent in Simon's room. She gave him a fast, hard but abbreviated massage. Her forearms ached, but it was a good feeling. She had given poor old Simon a lavish workout. Strange how a man so withered could have such a grand erection, when every other part of him was numb. Was that remnant of life just displayed for her, or had Sandy witnessed that same anomaly? No one must ever know what a foolish thing Connie had just done and she would make sure her depravity stayed secret.

Simon struggled as Curly, the Green Bay Packer's Physical Therapist manipulated his cramped thigh muscles, injured from smothering sack by the Viking's un-stoppable tackle, Allen Page. For three succesive plays his out-classed center four had been easily mowed down, leaving him un-protected and sacked. Less than twenty seconds in the game and his long scrambling run had brought his Packers within two points of winning the NFL championship.

On the forty yard line, the Packers were still ten yards short of their star field goal kicker's range and it was the fourth down. The trainer had to resurrect Simon, the oldest active quarterback in the league and get him in the game to produce a miracle.

Connie exited Simon's room as his daughter checked in at the reception desk. Head Nurse Keaghan personally escorted the nervous young woman to Simon's room, opened the door in a proud and proprietary manner, then left Linda Ware alone with her father for the first time in ten years.

Simon swung his feet around to the floor, and staggered to his best version of attention, a stance hampered by his smashed back. Although his Arab captors had not tortured him further, after his session on their interrogation rack had exploded the third thoracic vertebra, with an audible crack. That terminated his questioning and granted a five day respite, just long enough for him to heal and effectuate his escape.

He saw Golda, surrounded by security and reporters, approaching his stretcher with her nation"s highest honor in her hand. While she draped that ribbon and medal around his neck, Simon thought quickly of the speech, he must make, wondering how he could term his heroic acts of the past week into modest words, "Just doing my duty, Madam President".

Margo let down Simon's head and placed the gold cross on her father's chest. She had managed to encircle the fine cold chain around his neck without succumbing to temptation of winding it tightly, not from compassion, but of fear it would only break before strangulation occurred.

Her mother had never removed the cross, but when the mortuary director had asked whether Margo wished to keep her mother's jewelry, she remembered her mother' last request. She was here now to fulfill that wish. The Nurse had said that her father was dead by all standards, and had nothing left to live for. Margo delighted that her erstwhile father was blivious to his surroundings and unaware of the world around him.

Margo knew her father was unable to understand, were she to castigate him for all the years that he had abandoned her and her Mother. He was not able to see the disrespect, nay hate, that was in her eyes. How inappropriate was this religious symbol she had draped around her Father's neck. She had promised her mother that her failed, disappointing husband would wear the crucifix when he was laid to rest. Margo had bequeathed him that symbol of faith. Futile perhaps, as he was beyond help, unable to pray even if he had miraculously found faith while on the streets or while sobering up at some church mission. Calculating quickly, Margo realized her father was eighty-four years old and abusing his body with smoke and drink all the time she knew him. Why did he continue to hang on, while the woman he abandoned with three small children to raise, died still hoping for his return.

If she thought he could feel pain she would award him for his bounty for the deeds he had done. Her father's shameful life was over. Margo turned, and left still unable to summon up pity or hate for the man who had been her father.

Two hours later, Simon had a mystery visitor. Angry hands removed a pillow from his head, letting his head flop back, causing an involuntary but wry smile to form on his mouth.

Simon turned toward his accusers and grinned. "May the condemned man have one last cigarette?" A lit cigarette was placed between his lips and he sucked deeply, then tried to exhale. Nothing came from his lungs while the blindfold dropped over unseeing eyes.

Seven guns fired but only one was loaded with a blank. Simon Ware stopped breathing just before noon. Of all the many casualties at Sheltered Arms, Simon was the first death by a firing squad.

PICK OF THE LITTER

Elizabeth enjoyed visits to the farm of her mother"s parents, but she was aware this trip was very different. Everyone was sad, even her funny Uncle Jeff, who drove down to the city to get her. She waited on the big front porch steps, hoping her mother would surprise her by driving down, too. That of course, would be great news as that would mean she was finally getting better. She watched her grandfather coming from the mail box at the end of the farm driveway, looking very sad and walking especially slow, unlike his usual happy manner.

Yet, he said, "You look like you need a friend, Bethy. How about taking care of a new puppy? They're almost as friendly as Grandpas."

"Oh silly Gramps, you know Mommy won't allow dogs in our little apartment, with all the doctoring stuff, there. She always says dogs should live outside, like on farms, Grandpa"

"Well, some things are different now, Beth. Shag, our faithful old cow dog surprised us and had puppies and you will be living here on the farm until your Mommy gets better. I think Mommy wants you to have something special to love."

"Does Mommy know?"

"Yep, she told me that you can keep one of Shag's puppies, but just one."

"Will I be able to take my puppy back to our apartment, when Mommy leaves the hospital?"

"I just can't say for sure, Bethy. You know nothing is for sure and we don't know what tomorrow will bring. Let"s just say that you can have one of these puppies all the time you are here and it will be yours for a long, long time."

"Did Mommy really say I can have a puppy of my own?"

"Well, she didn"t say you couldn't and that is enough. I"ve got Shag's puppies in the barn. I"ll bring their box, so you can pick out the one you want."

Grandpa left her sitting on the front porch of the big old

farm house where he and Grandma lived alone, and went to the barn where he used to keep his milk cows before Grandpa and the cows got too old to take care of each other. She waited patiently with Mandy, her sort of sister and favorite doll. "Would you like us to have a puppy, Mandy?" Mandy never answered, but when you don"t have a daddy or any brothers or sisters, it was good to have someone who always listened. She knew Mandy would have said yes, as she had told her many times, how much she wanted a real live dog.

Her mother's father, her only grandfather, was soon back carrying a large corrugated paper box that said Eggs on the side. There were funny whimpering sounds coming from inside the box.

"Here are all four of Shag's puppies, Beth. They don't even have their eyes open yet. They are very hungry but Shag can't feed them, any longer."

"Where is Shag? How come she isn't with her puppies?" She had missed Shag when Uncle Jeff had delivered to her Grandpa's farm earlier that day. Shag always came running to play always carrying an old tennis ball in her mouth, whenever Beth stayed with her grandparents.

"She is old and very sick from having her puppies. You know, I don't have cows anymore and she misses her chores. Shag is really a sheepdog and she probably needs to get back to shepherding with her first master. All of us have this good friend who is a magnificent shepherd, and he has asked Shag to come help him, so Grandma and I have to take care of her puppies. We will soon feed them again and you can help."

"Well, why isn't Shag here? She didn't come to meet me. She always loves to play with me."

"She is resting. Grandma thinks Shag's new 'Master Shepherd' will be coming for her during the night. He will want to take her puppies with her but Shag will be glad to leave one with you."

"Do you mean Shag is going to die?"

"I guess, maybe. I think that you have to help her care for her baby. Which one are you going to pick."

"Oh Grandpa, they are all so cuddly. Look they try to eat my finger."

"Choose one and it will be yours. I've got to go help Grandma get your bedroom ready, so you take your time, pick out which one you want."

"When I go back to school in the fall, I will be going all day in the first grade. Can my new puppy have a puppy too? So he won't be lonely?"

"I am sorry, Bethy. You can only save one. The others must go shepherding with Shag."

"Can Mandy help me choose, Grandpa? Can I take them out of the box so she can see them too?"

"Yes, but very carefully and just one at a time"

"What kind of puppies, are they Grandpa?"

"We don"t know, but probably a very big dog. I would guess the father was a Great Dane. I would call them a Australian sheep dog and Great Dane hybrid."

"Would they bark in Dane or Australian, Grandpa?"

"Most likely, they would bark in dog language. We have to learn their language to talk to Dogs, Beth."

Just as Elizabeth reached for the mostly black puppy, the phone inside the farmhouse rang, causing Beth to lose her grip, and the puppy dropped back on its litter mates, causing puppy pandemonium. Grandpa came back with the portable phone and passed it to Beth. "Your mother is on the phone, honey. I told her you were picking out your puppy, and she was glad."

"Elizabeth, are you taking good care of Grandma and Grandpa, like you promised Uncle Jeff?"

"Is that really you, Mommy? Your voice sounds so strange. Does that strong medicine you have to take, make you sound funny?

"Mother is very tired, just now, Beth. Maybe tomorrow I will be better. Take good care of my Mommy and Daddy, sweetheart. Don't let them be sad and lonely, Okay? Tell them I do wish I could be there too."

"How long before you do come here, Mommy?"

"I will be coming to the farm very soon, Bethy. I want you to understand why, before I come."

"Mommy, Grandpa says I have to help him take care of Shag's puppies, but he says only one will stay here. I like the one with the spotty white hair, just like yours, Momma."

"Not anymore, Bethy. Right now I'm as bald as your grandpa. You would probably laugh at me, if I was there."

"I don't care if you don't look like my puppy. Anyway, I remember your hair was the same as my new puppy. What should I name it."

"Is it a girl or boy puppy, Beth?"
"I can't tell but I guess it doesn't matter. I want a name that doesn't care."

"When I was a little girl, your grandpa called me Sugar. I liked that. Would you like to name your dog the same as Mommy."

"Oh that's a sweet name. Won't that cause problems trouble when you come, Mommy? You won't know who I'm calling."

"It won't be a problem, Honey. I will always know when you want me. I would be proud of you choosing my old nickname for your dog. Your puppy will be an orphan, Beth, and orphans need super special love."

"Mommy, Uncle Jeff told Grandpa that he drove you to a hospice, before we came. Can we keep a dog in a hospice?"

"You won't be living in a hospice, Honey. That's just for your Mommy and just for a little while longer. You can stay on Grandpa's farm until you and your dog are used to each other. It will be a nice place for your dog, and you too!"

"Mommy, I'm so glad you changed your mind about dogs. I'm picking the puppy that likes me most and call it Sugar. I can hardly wait to bring him home."

"You just got there, Beth. Please do not hurt your Grandpa and Grandma's feelings by wanting to leave right away. Right now, they need you more than your Mommy does."

"But Mommy, I miss you so much!"

"You will like it there on the farm, won't you? I always did when I was your age. Have Grandpa show you all the places that made me happy. If you are in my favorite places, I bet we will be real close, like magic."

"Mommy, why are you crying?"

"I guess I miss you, Bethy. If I was there, I would show you and your new puppy, the trail to Willow creek. It's just a little way down the cow pasture lane. Back by those beautiful weeping willows. That's where the family graveyard is."

"How come you can't get well, here with us, Mommy? There's enough room for all of us."

"Sometimes people don't ever get well, Beth. I am writing you some letters, and ask Grandpa or Grandma to help you understand. Just remember that where ever you are, some part of me will be there too."

"Momma, are you going to die, too? Are you afraid to tell me goodbye?"

RESURRECTION

EkDDmLD3, Senior Ethicist, World Federation Population Control, still felt extremely tense and wondered why. He filliped twice to shut off the suddenly ineffective shock exerciser which usually twitched stressed muscles, relieving mental stress. He reached to the stem of his glasses for the control of his implanted computer and switched from reality so that his LaserBody performed as his worldly presence. In the public function mode, he was only a spectator of his life as projected on the official media screen. Ek took comfort knowing that the ethereal image of him being actualized, projected concern, politeness and political correctness. That correctness was assured by of constant monitoring by right-thinking officials of UPTC, Unified Public Thought Control. Much better, than he could of his own volition. Citizens asked questions that he did not have answers for and official doublespeak did not always satisfy a curious and increasingly demanding public.

At Anaheim, his laser bod was being introduced, and he said, "Hey, fine job, man." and was rewarded, as his public image came on his Compuglasses and winked back. Ek wondered how confident his stand-in would be if he knew how many of the attendees he was addressing were only Bods, too. Maybe his Little d was not always real. Who would know?   Maybe a session on his home compartment's antique exercise machine might ease his tension, but only if he could ignore his newly discovered allergy to the two dozen strawberry plants set in his home gym's wall. The fruity aroma only provoked bronchial spasms during heavy breathing, and thank Kosmos, he had tomato plants in the sleeping half of his home. He had applied for variance and specie change, medical basis, on his air purifier assessment but in spite of his level 3 social value, had not obtained audience space with the Cyprus Air Purity Control. It would probably help if he were to subscribe to a larger stock investment in Kosmos Corporation.

The mural in front of his console was still "Dawn over the

Aegean", the blue waters re-digitized from eighty years ago when the Mediterranean stretched from the Gibralter Dam to the gigantic fresh water iceberg admitting Locks of Suez. Soon, he would switch the screen to the Seaside Resort at Orlando Key where Ek, watch his LaserBod rise to begin his 'Welcome' speech to the lucky survivor of the Cryogenics Pool. Maybe the stress he still felt was due to the scheduled live interfacing with the press presences after his obviously well prepared vocal script. Unless, of course, there was heavy editing of that script not yet back from POCK, the Policy Overview Computerized Kosmos, who were the final interpreters of the world governing corporation. Ek had drafted the speech following corporate guidelines, but often policy changed during the course of a short speech.

Reincarnation in an overcrowded world was a sensitive issue and citizens struggling with rationed drinking water and severely polluted air, did not welcome people who extended their stay, and worse, came back from the dead. Except, of course, for themselves. A good reason to provide that one in ten-billion hope. The reincarnation lotteries were far more popular than the hourly money lotteries.

His personal wish had been to bring more of the CryoCrypt people to life, however he did not care to have Population Control publicly rebuke him again. Everyone is entitled to one mistake, but his last had been a whopper. As a consequence of his blunder, all of the remaining preserved specimens were now tested and certified ethnically correct, or destroyed. The fear of Superiorists still existed two hundred years after the great religious wars that had cratered the mid-east. Too bad some of the crypto-casques cancelled hadn"t been filled with more worthy but now extinct animals, rather than greedy and predatory humans.

Neither PC or Kosmos would ever take a controversial public stand, and his role seemed to be as designated goat. Ek was a certified slave descendant, though only on one genetic path, and rated even higher privilege placement. At least 4 and possibly 5, he figured. Ek checked the fact projector data bank for the third time and the format screen on his glasses correctly lit and flashed messages, at least in test mode. He would not risk mis-statement again, having previously interjected his belief that some live specimens should be retained in the Animal Life Museum. when instructed to defend the United Council's decision to substitute non-polluting, non-consuming Disney animation.

Had Ek not successfully blamed reflected inner glare on his reality-glasses for canceling his override message, the status administrator might have dropped him to social class three, and coupled with the trace of twinning genetic trait, be more vulnerable to cancellation of their birthing application. Without that, little d might truly regret pairing or even consider petitioning for re-shuffling, as she had potential value to reach class 3 herself. Ah yes, now he knew why the muscles in his back were still tight despite two sessions of electron stimulation in his console lounger.

Ek wondered if 'little d', his treasured life mate would tune him in from her office in TRAK, and somewhat resented that she signed in with Work Control while knowing that he was just up eleven levels, almost directly over their home compartment. Her work station was only seven point six minutes away by the transit tube. The tube caching, inevitable at Five AM when dawn shift workers were in passage, easily would stretch the time to work by another hour. Somehow, the possibility that he would need her support seemed likely. The nagging 'transmit count' buzzer sounded, so he hit view, and placed his right hand along the 'response trigger' on the body of his glasses and listened to his own voice simulation through his LaserBody begin....

"Citizeni, Citizena and Citizenoos of Kosmos, welcome to this historic event. Here, where billions of World Federation citizenry come to tour the Fountains of Youth Museum and where you, the lucky lottery winners of extended life are licensed, will probably all agree that this is a one happy place. Here where the smog is burned away by the bright light from Disney's newly launched Satellite Star, miracles are common. Today. you will make one of our dear departed very lucky. In a crowding world, citizenry has had to make many sacrifices, and we think it appropriate that our beloved Federation should occasionally reward you stockholders for your sacrifices. Here where our scientists at MAYO MEDICAL have learned how to double man's natural life span. Here where Disney Replication Studios have replaced the wild life in zoos with Animatee. Animal forms even more natural than real animals which consume victim-life to selfishly survive, pollute our precious and limited air with methane, our waters with polluting nitrates and set a bad example to our precious replacement kin. Here where your Federation has built this magnificent MUSEUM OF PAST LIFE where more than 1,000,000 life-worthy humans from the past await re-incarnation, preserved in Cocoons Of Liquid Argon. You will pick one of our ancestors to join us!!

"All of you are probably here because you value life. You know how precious is that gift! We will bring to life one, and only one, of the encrypted mementos of the past Ethnic Cleansing when our world was so minimally populated. When computers were external and uncontrolled purveyors of hate and indiscriminate passions. A time when people wasted resources, poisoned their environment and killed each other, because of their eye color or the God the worshiped. They, of course, perished by their excesses, and instead of a multitude of Gods, we now know with certainty that none exist.

Here before us, we have six cryo-preserved specimens. You have their bios in your program. As the head Crypt keeper places his pointer on the container, your recorded applause will select the one survivor," and then came the flash on the inner lowside of his glasses. Two quick green flashes, and an addition, probably previously decided but timed to appear impulsive. He looked to the camera, jammed the response button and dutifully read. "Your applause has chosen crypt three for resuscitation and your wish will be honored. In just two orbits, we will welcome Citizen CCkdBD9 back to our world and I will personally pledge to recondition BD, frozen at thirty-three but three hundred and sixty three years old."

A single green, pulsing digit, and he was back at his prepared presentation intoning, expansively, "It will be my personal task to acclimate this barbarian of the past, to our super-civilized society, to hold his hand while he is implanted with his life span license, which the federation has granted neutralization for two thirds of the time he was in suspended animation."

Three flashing red lights, his scripto-screen evaporated. "Oh my Emptiness," he blurted on his own, as if the Great Nothing would help him deal with total collapse of Federation Plan while even his LaserBody stood transfixed as Crypt 3 twitched, alternately swelled and glowed, in contradiction to all Einsteins. Then the screen in his glasses displayed green, and a new prompt.

He began to read, AThere has been a minor whitey, and we will have to re-choose. Our monitors indicate we have total de-ionization of the contents of Crypt three, yet the weight remains the same, indicating replacement with strange matter. The other candidates are equally..." He was silenced as he watched his Laserbody animation fall to his knees. His Compu-glasses overheated and burned his temples, but Ek dare not remove them, fearing what his LaserBody would say or do. Someone else was in control and that realization rought fear and a suspicion that the Federation was now in process of terminating him.

The lid lifted on Crypt three, and a figure arose. Ek zoomed in that figure and saw a smallish bearded man, quite thin and near naked except for a white breech cloth. His eyes were barely open as he lifted both hands high as in victory or to summon attention. Ek noticed a black crown of thorns around his head, and blood oozing from holes in both in his up-raised palms and from a gash in his side. Around his head was a green wreath, tinged with red. In stark contrast, his skin was gray, not black! Was it a practical joke from someone substituting a virtual but fictitious image, exploiting his sometime fascination with American mythology? EK had revealed that interest or knowledge in a bawdy white-faced parody of the greatest black hero and Federation Founder, 1A1, as part of the Ethnic Repudiation on War's End Day. Or was it another of his assistant's spurious machinations, a tactical trick to create his vacancy and replace him.

The only Whiteys anywhere in the Kosmos were but mechanizations in museums and the dioramas in Hate Centers. Ek could deal with the possible failure to resuscitate one of long-deads, but not the misinterpreted reading of the DNA aura scanned always before resuscitation. There was no possible way to resurrect anyone with traces of the still dreaded white man, years after War Crimes Commission had sterilized the few survivors of the great war. How could he ever explain this mistake, and why was his surrogate LaserBod rejecting his control, and welcoming a white man, scourge of the Federation and Universe? Creatures erased centuries ago.

EK knew he was not anyway responsible for this aberration but he knew, he would be held accountable. Like his LaserBody, Ek dropped to his knees and prayed to The Great Nothingness for answers. "Duck! Play dead, hide!" he mumbled to his surrogate LaserBod, but knew his advice was futile, even if received Through his earpiece, he heard one pained voice from POK control screech, "Oh, My Great Nothingness! He is one of those long-deads. An effen whitey!"

SQUAWMAN'S TEARS

Six and one half feet of Randall McQuirt, recoiled from his chair-tilting scrawl and concentrated on his nemesis, Jeb Steward's words. Jeb sounded a lot less frightened now than last night during his panicky flight from Randall and his troupe of Halloween pranksters. Randy reveled at the memory of his adversary, quaking in terror, as his marauders stormed through and destroyed Jeb's 'Pretend I'm an Indian' campsite.

Randy detested Jeb, not only because he was a rival for Shattuck Prep School's valuable and prestigious World Villager Scholarship, but because Jeb did not show proper deference to or fear of Shattuck"s star athlete, unlike the other fifty-eight seniors eligible for the Clinton Huber Founder's Award. Jeb had further antagonized Randy when Jeb applied for and won approval from Minnesota's Department of Natural Resources to create an authentic Indian Campsite in nearby Nerstrand Woods. That state forest land and little used State Park had provided Jeb Stewart a sociological lab that Randy's Instructors often recognized and enthusiastically endorsed.

Randy thought it another unfair benefit awarded minorities since Jeb used his claimed quarter Indian heritage whenever that seemed advantageous. Yet, he was not proud enough of his heritage to take an Indian name so Randy supplied one for him. Randy referred to his nemesis as Squawman and his campaign to discredit Jeb had netted him only two active partisans.

Those two loyal followers Gibson 'Pudge' Wainwringer, III and Holden 'Holly' Gibworth, had reluctantly joined Randy in his vigilante brigade the previous evening. Riding 'borrowed' horses from the school's stable, they had charged 'war-hooping' through Jeb's camp site clearing as their contribution to Faribault's Halloween madness. Riding abreast with a taut rope connecting the saddle pommels, Randy and Pudge straddled Jeb's teepee on their mad charge, toppling it over. Their only regret was not having brought a trumpet for their charge or night vision cameras to record the mayhem.

Jeb, rudely awakened had managed but feigned bravado, yelling to the departing riders, "Cowboy Cowards, come back and get decorated for your courage. Let me see your faces and I'll see that Custer shares his medals with you!"

Brave talk, but Jeb did scamper to the shelter of his old Volkswagen Beetle, and likely spent the night sleeping sitting, cramped in the questionable protection of a thirty year old car. Damned poor substitute for a war horse, Randall thought. Jeb seemed to be nursing a stiff neck and his eyes looked puffy indicating the raiders had destroyed Jeb's sleep. Randall listened intently, not that he was really interested in another report on the typical indian diet and social structure as reported by the faux indian, but for Jeb's reaction to his raiders.

The weekly reading from Jeb's journal was often Friday fare in Dr. Karl Haymen's Sociology Class, unfairly giving importance to the experiment, whereas Randall's project on the 'Birth of Leadership' was given short shift, and mostly ignored.

Randall's rapt attention was rewarded. Jeb Stewart had decided to report last night's calvary charge. Had Stewart recognized the interlopers? No matter. Randall knew he was too popular to be condemned or ostracized by the student body. His parent's would not be at all stressed financing his college education were he to forfeit the prized scholarship.

"Last night a cowardly band of Custer's Ghosts sought revenge against me, a descendant of their adversary, the victorious Ogalala Sioux. My teepee was destroyed, my artifacts trampled, my store of dried fruits and vegetables strewn in the dirt and my journal scattered in the wind. The contemptible attackers must never return for they will not have the protection of surprise. My Amerind ancestors trusted the white man and believed his pledges, but once! I too, unwisely trusted my white neighbors and suffered pain and injury. I have no tears for Indians never cry. Nor will I have sympathy for those who perish in the storms they create. I give this warning to the masked cowards! Do not return to the grounds of Squawman, for it will be as dangerous as the bluffs of the Little Big Horn."

Not waiting for the usual applause of the, Jeb abruptly sat in his assigned chair, while the class collectively and ominously held their breath. Did friendly, scholarly and usually timid Jeb Stewart become so engrossed in his project that he turned completely Indian? If so, why did he choose such an ugly and degrading name as Squawman. After a painfully long and silent interval, Professor Haymen rose to dismiss the class.

Surprising himself, Randall also rose and when all eyes were focused on him, spoke theatrically, "White men, beware the wrath of the Squawman!" He turned to his flanking seat companions, the ashen faced Gibson Wainwright and nervously blushing Holden Gibworth and softly pledged, "Tonight we will see if Indians cry."

Jeb Stewart skipped his last hour, Physical Education class, aware it was merged with basketball try-outs where his scrawny and poorly coordinated, slightly short of six feet physique, would not be missed. Randall would be there, basking in the glory his stature merited. Randall's outburst had confirmed that he had engineered last night"s humiliating raid on his camp.

After stopping at the Hometown Hardware for sign supplies, Jeb hurriedly and recklessly drove the twelve mile route from Shattuck Academy Campus, to Nerstrand State Park, swerving dangerously on the last two miles of gravel. His faithful old Volkswagen shimmied like a belly-dancer. The bug had goosey steering from worn out front axle bushings Jeb usually appeased by slow and careful driving. Jeb had much to do before this evening's expected visitors.

First, Jeb painted two signs with blazing red flourescent paint on dull black poster boards with the dire warning, 'BEWARE! Trespassers are in mortal danger! Deadly Force Awaits Any Intruders". Jeb needed one for each end of the steeply sloping creek valley he considered his domain. He had a battery lantern for both entrances, though only the drive-way near his camp site was accessible by vehicles. Here, fifty yards from his teepee, he parked his beetle and this was where last night's invading rowdies had began their charge. Jeb hung the first sign, lit by the lantern and hung from the cable where that driveway ended.

Jeb expected his no longer anonymous attackers, provoked by his warning, would come down the upper end of Prairie Creek, probably parking where the creek passed through the culvert under Highway 27. The way was steep and treacherous but there was a pathway of sorts, precariously following the steeply descending creek bed, through heavy timber and brush to where it widened into his clearing. Halfway down that half mile trail, a natural gas pipeline crossed the creek bed. There, he hung the other lantern and sign. If his sneaky brigands returned, it would be tonight. Tomorrow, their motivations would cool, and he could take down the signs and disarm his defenses.

The cowardly marauders had awakened feelings Jeb Stewart had never experienced. For the first time, he felt complete kinship with his Indian ancestors, no longer just an amateur anthropologist focused on downtrodden and much victimized losers. He could taste their defeats and was hungry for vindication.

Fifty feet from his ethnically correct garden, where the narrow creek valley first widened and the steep course of Prairie Creek flattened, a thick, virtually impenetrable stand of tall and supple poplars crowded both sides of the narrow trail. Here, Jeb prepared his ambush, just as described in Goodlink's 'Lore of the Woodland Indian.'

Jeb shinnied up one poplar almost half a foot in diameter, chopping free enough of the branches to clear passage to the thin and compliant top. Jeb swivelled and twisted until he had the tree bent in direct line-up with the trail, but he still dangled ten feet off the ground. Clasping the now horizontal tree trunk with his legs, he managed to fasten his length of rope, securing with a slip knot woven around a larger forking branch. Jeb groped about and found the trunk of a neighboring poplar. With much difficulty, he managed to tie his rope to the tree without sacrifice of the bowed tree"s upward tension. The bent tree's tip was still ten feet above the ground, and needed more weight.

From his crumpled tent, Jeb took his wash tub, and attached tip, loading it with stones until the tub touched the ground. The arched tree provided more than ample spring for his snare. While fashioning the hair-trigger latch and release, Jeb clumsily slipped the knife blade into the web of his thumb. Stanching the bloody wound in his mouth, he tasted his blood and found it stimulating, finally explaining for him the blood-letting portion of the secret Sioux Death dance.

Two hours later, he sat by his campfire, prepared for marauders. Twenty feet beyond his first snare, Jeb had rigged another ambush. A second, smaller but more painful, bowed branch bearing a sharpened lance rigged to swing in a horizontal plane. The sharpened stake, lashed with authentic rawhide to the fork at the tip of the tensed beech sapling protruding but two inches beyond it"s attachment. Not deep enough to cause death when it snapped forward, buttocks high, into the rear of any interloper who could not avoid his ankle high, hair-trigger trip. While his campfire turned to embers, Jeb finished his cattail root and roasted acorn soup, almost authentic except for the stew beef from Swiggen' Bargain Foods as a necessary substitute for venison.

In spite of his cropped red hair and freckles, Jeb felt like a Sioux Warrior. He filled the empty hand-pinched and ash fired bowl with creek water and poured it into the fire pit, safely extinguishing all embers. He snuggled feet first under the edge of his still crushed teepee, and into his imitation bear skin bed. His uncovered head allowed Jeb to check both of his north and south campsite entrances. Jeb could see some light from both lanterns illuminating his dire warnings. 'Squawman' was ready but his tormentors might more accurately call him 'Prepared Porcupine'.

Soon they came, conspiring with whispers dying in the cool, crisp early November air. Fortified by a six pack of beer and armed with a shotgun and two cans of gas, the potential arsonists drove in Pudge's Porsche to the campground entrance. There, they quickly snatched open the hood of Jeb"s ancient Volkswagon. Working quickly and following their erstwhile leader's plan, they removed the distributor cap and took it with them.

The invaders could see the dim light of the warning lantern further up the trail and Holly whispered, "He's waiting for us. Let's do this another night, Randy."

Striding toward the light, Randy saw the warning signs and was not intimidated. "Hey look, he's trying to intimidate us. Read the sign, and laugh." Pudge and Holly did not laugh.

Away in their car, silence was abandoned. Randy sang loudly, "I don"t care if I do die, do die. Tonight I"ll see my Squawman cry", over and over until even his loyal henchmen tired of its cleverness. Both quietly concluded Randy had overdone his persecution but not enough to challenge their leader's judgement.

When they reached the culvert on Highway 27, at the headwaters of Prairie Creek, silence was resumed. Parking just beyond the creek, they pulled stealthily into an abandoned driveway that had once had been a cultivated farm field. Before becoming a state park, parts of Nerstrand Woods had been cleared for farming but none of the rugged portion had been tamed and remained as it was when Columbus landed, frightening even during daylight.

The returning marauders were dressed totally in black, with faces distorted by the toe-end remnants of newly bought black panty hose. An embarrassing preparation and purchase that Randy had delegated to Holly Gibworth.

Randy led them down the ravine, carrying his father's prized shotgun, and a small two cell flashlight. Pudge and Holly carried the heavy gas cans and, without more light, were left to guess safe foot placement on steeply descending creek bank, heavy with underbrush and littered with loose stones.

"It's too hard walking here in the dark," Pudge softly protested, "Let's go in the other way, Please Randy."

"This is the only way we will take him by surprise. Squaw man won't think we would ever make it this way, and that's our element of surprise. Besides, we need the wind at our back. Now shut up and look down at my feet where I need to keep the light. The beam goes up once, he'll know were coming. That's why I"m carrying the light! No more noise, now! Step slowly and carefully"

The marauders were not surprised to encounter the second lantern lit warning sign, hung from the pipe line crossing the creek. It was identical to the sign at the other end of Jeb Stewart's camp. Randy was not deterred. He confidently whispered to his lagging companions. "Oh man, he must be really scared. This will be fun. We'll have Squawman looking for an Indian Reservation to camp on. He'll send his journals in to Doc Haymen by smoke signals!"

Bravely striding forward, even benefitting by the warning lantern's light on the lushly verdant trail, Randy did not see the carefully placed and ready trip branch surreptitiously poised six inches above and parallel to the ground. He barely felt the resistance of that trip branch as he nudged it forward with his ankle. The branch unlatched from a carefully cut notch on a trail side scrub oak setting loose the peg tethering the bowed poplar trap. Randy had no time to ponder why that snagging branch was different from the others as a loop of rope gripped him around both ankles and snatched him skyward, feet first in a gigantic arc like the tip of an enormous bull whip. Randy was jerked away from the flashlight and shotgun which fell to the rocky trail. Randy's head was the tip of that cracked whip, stretching his spinal cord, leaving him temporarily paralyzed and dangling unconscious six feet above the trail. Randy's eyes were open but unseeing.

Holly crumpled forward wondering why his leader's errant shotgun had fired backward and why at his gut. Pudge grabbed Randy's falling flashlight and cowardly scrambled back toward the rugged and punishing trail to the security of his waiting car.

A real Sioux Indian would've smelled the coming intruders and heard their noisy descent down the trail. Jeb slept deeply and confidently unafraid until he heard Randy's abbreviated scream and the simultaneous blast from his dropped shot gun. Shocked awake, Steward grabbed his security light and his ceremonial hunting knife from under his rolled up bed roll and ran toward his oppressors. In the circle of his flashlight, he saw Holly on his knees, slumped forward, clutching his belly as if to stop the gushing blood and Randy hanging upside down and motionless.

Jeb roared, "What in Hell happened here?" He pulled down on Randy's inanimate body until the head and shoulders touched the ground and cut the suspending rope which twanged away. His snared victim's body collapsed to the ground and lay unmoving. "Is he dead?" Jeb asked the shadows, as he checked Randy's feeble, yet discernible pulse.

Then Jeb, adrenalin racing, easily picked up the bloody but still breathing Holly, who evidenced life by whimpering, "Help me, Randy. Please help me, please help me, Squawman."

Slung over his shoulder, Holly's bulk was manageable and Jeb lumbered to his car. He clumsily opened the door of his Beetle and transferred the barely breathing Holly to the passenger seat. With no way to place a tourniquet, Jeb could only hope to reach a hospital before Holly bled to death. Quickly racing to the driver's side and settling, Jeb turned the key. The starter whirred and whirred. In spite of the mainly miles it had traveled, it always faithfully started. He tried again but heard only the defeated sound of his baffled starter, spinning ineffectively. Jeb raced to the rear of the Volkswagen. Hood lifted, the dim light of his warning lantern showed the loose wires and a decapitated distributor.

Squawman leaned against his impotent wheeled warhorse, and tears of frustration filled his eyes and coursed down his cheeks. Randall McQuirt had done what he promised. He had made Squawman cry!

TARBABY

Ducking back into the darkened doorway, I watched Reverend Bill Haley look back toward Ball Street, then turn into the alley where my booby-trap waited. I thought a prayer, begging that no real bum had camped there. Haley, who founded the mission that last sheltered Oscar Fernandez would not find him there. He was secretly stashed in our 'drunk-tank'.

Normally, I'm very honest. I felt guilty telling Reverend Haley, that his missing lodger was spending nights under the freight delivery dock of Winkler Publishing. During yesterday's regular breakfast meeting, Haley had asked why the department wasn't more interested in Oscar? Didn't he fit the profile of the homeless men who were frequent victims of the serial killer my special task force targeted? Haley's concern seemed logical, even if phony, considering the current death toll of nine slumbering winos, clubbed into permanent sleep.

I let slip that Oscar hung out in the alley behind Winkler Printing, probably because a vent from a rotogravure oven diffused ethanol fumes almost like the atmosphere of the saloons that no longer tolerated Oscar's non-paying presence. We both laughed, and Bill did not suspect that I knew him to be the serial killer, or that I was setting him up.

Only eight of the killer's victims, all alcoholics bums and frequent residents of Haley's Mission had been done in by the characteristic single cranium crushing head blow. The reported body count of nine murdered street people actually included one indigent tramp sent to God"s mercy, courtesy of exposure and or liver failure. The Toledo Blade had unwittingly counted him too. We did not correct them. Far better that the true body count be known only to the killer and the police task force I headed.

I first suspected my friend and sponsor, Reverend Haley, because of his accurate count. Just a week ago, during the short funeral ceremony at Haley's East Street Mission for Harold Dunfrey, the killer's last victim, Reverend Haley referred to eight poor lost souls now sleeping on streets paved with gold, where there was neither pain nor hunger. The slip could easily be explained by a security breach from other officers, who like myself, often shared confidences with their old friend and ex-policeman turned chaplain.

The indisputable proof of Haley's guilt came exclusively to me the day before yesterday while I was at Bill's office for a coffee break. We were pleasantly chatting in his office until he was called away to mediate a tiff in the second floor dormitory between two late sleeping guests. Bill's interrupted work lay before me. I can still see the scrawled notes in Haley's sloppy handwriting that only I, among Bill's close associates, could decipher. Haley had a brief outline of a planned funeral oration with a skimpy biography of Oscar Hernandez.

Haley's described Hernandez as, "A proud father and successful businessman, who had been weak and fell on bad times but now would be sauntering down the Streets of Gold, in God's heavenly kingdom."

Silently keeping that secret for the rest of the day was the worst burden I ever faced since joining the police force almost fifteen years ago. Getting me decked in patrolman blue was another of the many times Bill Haley had gone to bat for me. I could not share my shocking discovery with anyone, duty be damned.

Nor could I let a killer's murderous rampage continue, no matter who or how important he might be. During that night's sleepless tossing, I hatched a solution that did not include breaching the invisible wall of blue or further destruction of his good name. Bubby, my baby-sitting older brother had read to me, all of the Uncle Remus stories.

My favorite was about a rabbit who destroyed an evil fox with his booby trapped tar baby, and that treasured fable suggested the best solution. I began creating my own booby trap, that next morning. Getting enough dynamite and the touchy fulminate of mercury primer surreptitiously from the property room had been risky, but easy. I created a passable, at least in the dark, replica of Oscar from a mannikin that had once been a CPR training dummy at the Fourth Street Fire House, and I hoped, untraceable. After all, it had languished the past five years in my basement. My brother had brought it over, with a bawdy legend painted on her belly.

That was ribald humor unlike my solemn and proper brother, but intended to make light of my wife"s leaving. Only my brother knew I still had the dummy secreted in the basement as another reminder of my failure as husband and father. My brother would have never revealed its existence, since he knew how much it embarrassed me.

When the 'bum killer', found my Oscar and lashed out again with his signatory, 'One quick blow to the head,' he too, would be in pieces, torn apart by two sticks of dynamite. I had broken up the waxy sticks and mixed the doughy mass of dynamite with a quarter pound of fulminate of mercury stolen from the property room. This potent mess I had packed in the mannikin's plastic head. The manikin's body, dressed in old and dirty clothing from the jail's lost and found bins even wearing the real Oscar's ratty old trench coat, transformed that once lovely teaching aid into a representation of Hernandez, but only for a quick and impetuous look in poor light.

I parked my car two blocks away as a necessary precaution, as it had often been used by Bill Haley, when I had tried to repay his many favors. My presence where Haley sought Oscar would tell him that I knew his secret.

Nervously counting, I was timing Haley's walk to the booby trap. After counting to thirty-eight with no explosion, sweat began to soak my armpits. Had Bill tried talking to Oscar, and discovered my deadly trap? My nervous count reached fifty before a large explosion shook the ground. A pressure wave swept from the alley with the acrid smell of expanded nitrogen. Some alerted siren sounded nearby, and I waited just one more minute before running, out of breath, toward the blast scene. Even while running, I worried whether I left evidence that could tie me to Haley's execution? Did I leave clues or evidence for the investigators?

I might be caught but Haley deserved death. He must have fancied himself a mercy killer or deputy of God, but my vigilante action probably spared many more winos he would have killed had I followed procedure and only reported my suspicions. If not destroyed, Haley would eventually be caught, destroying the good part of his Christian mission and bringing shame on his family and their proud police heritage.

Now, I too was a murderer, like my victim, and also deserved execution despite undertaking a life-saving mission, but of winos not ranking high on social value. If caught, my only regret would how this might would reflect on my father's impeccable record. He too, had his wife leave him, and he tried to ruin his good name drowning his grief in booze, without help from me.

Dad's abused liver failed him almost a year ago, but finding out that his oldest son was a murderer, not an esteemed man of God would torture him, even in death. I alone, Officer Alston Haley, had killed my hero and devoted brother, Bubby. Maybe I could explain why when I would soon see him next, walking down his beloved Streets of Gold, in God's Heavenly Kingdom.

REFLECTED ME

In my mirror, when I look there,
  three very different men, I see.
The shiny one with the saintly air,
  is the man I'd like to be.
That sneering lout with angry stare,
  looms meanest of the three.
But the middle man, so meek and spare,

seems the one that's really me.

THE EXECUTIONER WAITS

Jean's eyes opened as the first rays of the new sun squeezed through the bars of the tiny window, high-up in the tall and narrow stone walled cell. Jean's closed eyes, blocking the bright rays, would not postpone the dawn with its inevitable summons by King Roderick's Royal Guard. Today"s execution was set for seven and would not be delayed. It had been a warm night but Jean shivered with apprehension. Visions of headless monsters, rising from the scummy moat that ringed Roderick's Castle haunted Jean the long fitful night. Last night"s recurring apparition was of a beautiful young girl in a blood stained but once white wedding gown, smeared with kitchen garbage and night-pot trappings, blindly grabbing at her mutilated neck as if searching for her missing head. She was not a stranger.

In the horrible dream, the macabre bride demanded Jean's head to replace her own. The apparition faded as Jean struggled awake but the beheaded bride had been real, and well remembered by Jean. A former favorite of King Roderick had been discarded, then decapitated after three years of honeymoon that had not provided an heir to the Plavonian Throne. Jean had attended that beheading at Roderick's command, but took no pleasure watching the axe blade stall halfway through the neck. Jean shuddered in shock as the unlucky executioner stood back, axe raided, considering a second swing to sever the small and beautiful neck.

As the young Queen's blood gushed from the first wound, the public throng squealed in excitement. The eyes of the former Queen closed and re-opened three times from pain or automatic reflex. Or had it been a signal or message to someone. Since that execution, Jean had continued to obsessively ponder that riddle.

The Royal executioner with the too soft swing would have probably gratefully suffered such a harsh fate, even from a dull axe requiring many strokes, rather than his certain tortured end in the King's dungeon. Unlike hangings and be-headings, torture was never witnessed by Roderick's subjects and Jean wondered why? Maybe, slow death was not interesting, even if it were a crueler deterrent to illegal behavior, but unwitnessed by the masses. Plavonia's citizens were to be taught by public example, that giving displeasure to the King was a capital crime.

When the doomed executioner botched the first swing of his axe, he had summoned help from the attending officials, but no one volunteered. Agonizing minutes passed while the lips of the discarded Queen tried to form words. Finally, King Roderick stepped forward and arrogantly grabbed the long, golden tresses of his former bride and stretched out her mutilated neck tightly over the chopping block, whether out of mercy or unwilling to imagine his Ex-Queen's final thoughts. Was she yet alive to feel that last insult? When did death occur? Blood slowly seeped from her severed head and yet the eyes stared knowingly.

Jean lay sleepless most of the night, agonizing over the unanswerable mysteries of execution by axe. How could the victim communicate with a disconnected head. Even if the tongue could form the words, where would the force of voice come from. The expelling air from the severed neck made bubbles and a slight hiss. How could someone make known how horrible death by axe felt, with unspoken testimony.

If only the crowd could feel some of the pain, and Rebuke the King by refusing to witness such a gory spectacle. Could their attendance mean they lacked compassion or was their participation only relief that it was not their neck on the block. Jean remembered witnessed many executions, but could not remember any proof of continuing pain. Maybe, swift death, allowed no pain at all, but who would tell.

Jean's painful contemplations were interrupted by the Captain of the King Roderick's Royal Guard, who rapped softly and politely on Jean's door, then muttered, "It is time, Jean, come with us."

The dreaded moment had arrived. Jean rose from his bed, praying, "Oh blade, be swift and well aimed. Spare Queen, Marianne from suffering." He reached for his axe that he had honed and re-honed during the last fitful night.

Dare he hope that this would be the last beautiful Queen Good King Roderick would condemn to death. Jean hoped that he would only have to watch, not do the execution of another beautiful girl cursed with the impossible task of providing a son for a seedless King Roderick.

INDIAN CORN
Dead Indians, embalmed with salt from unshed tears,
wait too patiently for the ghost dance drum beat.
I see them huddled in shadows when sun disappears
over the blood stained Buttes, where Custer met defeat.
The keening of slain children are what the wind hears
and amplifies to ripple the stubs of dry land wheat
tamed Sioux politely plant at the Little Big Horn
for baking white man's bread. Braves, now less despised,
hide two hundred and twenty six scalps and mourn
their dead in secret. Grandsons of those unrecognized,
still plot and plan when drunk on fermented corn,
full revenge for raids Custer considered civilized.

TRAVELING COMPANIONS

Clarence Bocker, born in poverty and injury afflicted, survived his hard life to host his ninety-third birthday. Two visitors came. James, his son and sole survivor who brought a package of Clarence's favorite bitter-sweet chocolate along with an expensive greeting card bearing best wishes. A surprise for the staff since James had not visited since the year before when he brought Clarence the confusing news of the death of Jame's mother, Rose. James had fumed ranted over Clarence's lack of grief over Rose and found it easier to put off of coming to see his father.

Nor did Clarence really recognize his son James except as the pesky fellow who had come around several times with an exceedingly old, fat and wrinkled lady that insisted on kissing him goodbye while crying messy tears. The pesky man, James had yelled, "THIS IS ROSE, YOUR WIFE, DON'T YOU REMEMBER ANYTHING?"

Clarence knew this was nonsense, and assured himself. "Rose is beautiful! This old lady is fat and wrinkled as a raisin. Rose's hair was golden as September corn tassels, not faded gray. Why is this old lady pretending to be my Rose?"

Rose gamely tried not to cry.. Tears were useless if they weren't seen or recognized. Stodgy and old, no longer like a young willow turning in the wind, Rose told her son, "Maybe it is best that Clarence only remembers me as young and beautiful."

Yes, Clarence's beautiful Rose had stopped coming years ago. James persistently tried to bring reality to his father, because Rose was failing and soon would be incapable of visiting. It did bother James that his father did not recognize him, his own son. James did not rationalize that Clarence did not recognize any of 'Silvertip Manor's nurses or staff who daily bathed, fed and humored Clarence. They were more conditioned to the anomaly of a healthy body hosting a brain that died early, stealthily inching toward oblivion one small loss each day.

Ah, but the other birthday visitor, Clarence immediately recognized. He had last seen his dear old friend Spot eighty years ago when they would fetch the cows from the pasture across the road for the evening milking. All Clarence would need to do was open the fence and Spot would eagerly and masterfully bound up the pasture toward the cows usually congregated at the pasture's far end where the creek had inspired a few shady cottonwoods. Clarence waited at the gate while his dependable cow dog brought all the cows to the lane, expertly nipping at the heels of the 'au courant' Boss Cow just enough to move the complacent followers.

At that very road crossing, he had said a tearful good-bye to his constant companion and best friend. Clarence remembered clearly his great sadness and profound guilt. Spot had stopped in the middle of the road, while a terrified Clarence on one side and his equally distraught father on the other, both calling for their endangered dog. Standing there, puzzled at opposing calls from his two masters, the always obedient and willing dog ignored the oncoming Model T Ford. The carload of city folk stopped and commiserated over Spot's death, but hastily left continuing their Sunday pleasure drive, mollified that they had proffered five dollars compensation, and been refused..

His Dad assured Clarence that Spot had not been confused by their simultaneous calls but instead, was waiting for one last straggling cow to safely cross. Clarence had wished the cow had been hit instead. A dead cow meant beef on the table, instead of stringy old hens too old to still lay eggs. Times were tough on that small Wisconsin dairy farm, but the family always ate, even if not too fancy.

Dad brought home a new Border Collie pup, from the same neighbors that had given them Spot. Clarence never even named him, calling him Pup, Shep or sometimes, just Dog. He too grew to be a reliable cow dog, didn't kill chickens or scare the sheep, but Clarence did not share his bed or tell secrets to this new dog regarding him as an unpaid farm worker too,.

His beloved Spot woke Clarence Bocker just after sunset, nuzzling his nose under his arm as of old. He was so thankful that Spot was again alive, relieving a lifetime of regrets about his guilt in Spot's tangle with that careless Model 'T' driver, that he leaped out his high hospital bed, like a young kid. Spot turned and trotted through the usually closed door to Clarence's room and on down the aisle toward the fire exit. "Taking the cows to the pasture, Spot? Have we already done the milking?" Clarence joyfully followed his long lost friend.

Snoring already came from several of the patient's room and one of the snorers must have been the night watchman as Clarence easily exited the fire door before the alarm sounded.

There beside the door shining in the yellow glow of the security light was a dead ringer for Clarence's first car. A shiny black 1936 Chevrolet Master Tudor just like the one he had once scrimped so hard to buy, convincing beautiful Rose that he was a man of means and would be a good provider. It looked to be the very same car he had used to court Rose Scargle, the prettiest girl in Beaver Falls and the only girl he ever loved. Clarence went directly to the familiar car and tried the driver's side door. The door was unlocked and the courtesy light revealed a passenger, waiting for him. It was his young and lovely Rose sitting regally in the passenger seat.

Clarence also noticed his old but remembered keys on his lucky rabbit foot ring in the ignition. His trusty dog Spot was already in the back seat. Clarence always knew Spot was smarter than any other dog, but how could his dog tell Rose which car to sit in. Clarence, too breathless to speak, only smiled at his Rose and she smiled back with that same beautiful smile he had always treasured. She was as radiant and lovely and wore the same white wedding gown she wore that wonderful day Pastor Enger pronounced them man and wife, making him the happiest man in all of Wisconsin..

Clarence grinned at Spot and Rose. When you have a long ways to go it's nice to take your best friends along. Clarence gently patted the Spot's head, smiled at the beautiful woman beside him, and turned the key eager to go wherever they were going.

Alzheimer's Endowment
My castle has been invaded,
the moat spanned and the walls breached.
Somewhere within
a prowler paws through my treasures,
purloining past and present.
Those precious gems of remembrances,
he sifts through with sticky fingers
and they disappear from view.
Capriciously, he teases me
with shadows of where they were.
This sneak thief will soon leave
taking away his every footprint.
I won't know he has stolen my name
and wiped away forever my oneness.
No longer aware of my loss,
will I be Victim or Victor?

THE WELL TAMPERED JURY

Bill Johnson wore that honest kind of face that some used car salesmen are blessed with. You know the kind. Look you in the eye, and tell you that a used car is in perfect condition when you know it is a wreck since you knew the previous owner and yet, you almost believe him. So I looked him in the eye and said, "This may seem more formal than it really is. Basically, you are giving testimony as if you were in a courtroom." Johnson nodded and sat where I had indicated, but nervously, like a hen setting down on eggs in the presence of a fox. I switched on my tape recorder.

I continued, smiling my friendliest 'out on campaign' smile, "Do you mind if I call you Bill while we tape our conversation, Mr Johnson?"

Bill slumped forward, finally settling with both forearms resting on the conference table in the District Attorney's most placidly disarming interview room, and drew a deep breath, before answering, "Call me anything you want, except guilty of a crime, Mr. Williams." He turned up both palms in a magnificent gesture of openness or expert coaching, and gruffly, spoke again, "You may infer this is just a procedural deposition, but you are preparing a statement for the Grand Jury, right?".

My gambit compromised, I changed gears and voice, then confided, "We don't like to lose any case, but when somebody confesses to a crime and the jury can't find her guilty of anything, we do look for excuses. Can't admit we did a lousy job of prosecution, can we?"

"No, I suppose not. Did you know that our first vote produced only one vote for acquittal?"

"Yes, I saw your tally sheets. There's twelve jurors, yet your tally shows thirteen. Who voted twice?. That's why we're here, man. We just need to get the facts."

Bill laughed, no sign of guilt showing. "I have been trying to figure that out since the trial ended. Talked to the other jurors, too and they are as puzzled as me. Be sure to question them, too."

"Well let's begin, Bill. Please speak clearly as my secretary is prone to guessing words, she don't catch. You get a chance to proof the statement, but let's make her job easier. No head nodding, Right?"

Bill nodded and in a friendlier and more trusting manner said, "Yes, I have nothing to hide."

I did all the customary preface, explaining the legal consequences of false testimony, gave a legal but paraphrased and slightly oblique Miranda warning and the due notice of recorded testimony. When I said, "It is the seventeenth of November, 2003 and I am County Attorney Brad Williams of Corker County, Minnesota. I am questioning Bill Johnson, of 631 Kelly Gardens, Weldone, Minnesota. Are you..."

"Bill laughed so hard, I stopped the tape. He knew I was Corker County's Chief Prosecutor as I had just finished proving beyond all shadow of doubt that Kristy Jane Willows caused the death of her unborn child. Bill Johnson came back to the court and said eleven other jurors besides himself, had found her innocent. In all of Corker County, there are not three citizens who would find her innocent.

Something rotten had happened in the sequestered jury room, and Bill Johnson was the foreman of the jury that made a mockery of justice. I had to find out who 'got to' the jury. "Did you volunteer to be the foreman, Mr. Johnson," I asked remembering that Johnson had been my favored choice of all the jurors seated. He was in favor or capital punishment, was a church deacon and had four children. Had I missed something? Bill answered, "Everyone picked their choice. I got six votes on the first round and that made me foreman. I sure as hell didn't volunteer. I got to live in this town."

"So, how come you counted twelve votes for conviction on your first tally, which sure as Hell is unanimous, but keep on voting for three days and end up finding for acquittal."

"I can't give you that answer. I learned to count before I was three and I've always been good with numbers. Do bowling averages in my head. I done the counting, as did ALL the jurors. We didn't see our count as twelve."

"Well, who was the only holdout on that first goofy count, then?"

"That was Chris. He made a great speech about perfection. Four jurors turned on the next count."

"Chris? We didn't seat any Chris. Chris who?" I had the detailed list of jurors right in front of me, and there wasn't anyone there entitled to called Chris.

Puzzled, Bill looked me in the eye, daring me to disbelieve. "You know, that beatnik looking fellow who wore the ragged long coat and spoke with a captivating bass voice. We all loved to hear him talk, even if he was dead wrong."

"The bailiff clocked you in and out. There were only twelve people in the jurors room, twelve beds slept in at the Cozy Inn, and never more than twelve meals brought in. There was no Chris."

"So you say, but ask Nancy Larson. She tallied all the counts, and she was the fiercest holdout for conviction. Everyone in the county is against abortion, but no one more zealous than Nancy. Don't know how you got her paneled, after she told you that rape was a lesser sin than killing the baby born of a rapist father."

"Yet Miss Willows walked after admitting she killed her baby, and you blame the innocent vote on someone who wasn't there."

'You weren't there with us, Mr. Williams. You would have seen him and counted him, too."

Now, I was angry, but held back, and patiently explained, "I wasted my time proving guilt beyond all shadow of doubt, and failed to convict. Remember, Miss Willows said, under oath, she stabbed herself, specifically to kill the baby!"

Bill spoke to me like I was the slowest student in his weekly Sunday School class. I sat over in the corner, where Chris talked with all the others. He told me a little story thing, I remember almost every word and I will never forget his message. It probably changed my vote. I know what he told me, but I don't know what he said to the others."

"Well tell me that sick story your jury ghost told you," I said courteously smothering my snickers.

With a straight face, Bill recounted what Chris had told him. "Bill said, 'Bill, I know you are religious man. You pray for driving skill each morning before you check out your school bus. I know you think the court must punish Miss Willows because she admitted killing her baby and several other sins, and yet she begs for forgiveness. Just let me tell you a little more about our God.

Everyone believes God is infallible, but this was not always true. In fact, God's first creation ended in total failure. That first world he made much like this one, except he wanted happy residents who could demand from their Creator, complete satisfaction of their every need. Their only duty was to glory in his handiwork. The first man complained that their world was sometimes too hot, while his female companion said it was far too cold. God tilted their world's orbit, and gave them too much of both. When the pair complained, God promised to fix their world with a less tilt and more averaging. Unsatisfied, the pair complained about the hardships of their landscape. The man thought the hills were too high and blocked his view. The woman complained about how deep the valleys were and impossible to cross. Eager to please, God flattened the hills, filled in the valleys making the Earth level as a pool table. The couple who hadn't learned to swim, drowned in the resulting flood when the oceans lost their retaining shores. We are fortunate that God resolved to forsake perfection, and tried again. Bob, how can we expect or demand perfection.' His story convinced me to change my vote."

"Bill, you are talking about an imaginary person that you've created, in your mind. Kids do that when they're alone too much. What is your excuse? Phantoms and fantasy. What did you gain by switching your vote?"

"Have you chosen me as goat because I was the last hold out for guilty? Nancy Larson was the last to change, you know. Before our last vote, she said, 'We must let God judge her sin.'"

Very noble abdication of duty, I thought. There was no good reason to continue questioning Bob. I needed to find that Chris, fellow. Maybe he could help me understand why there was a thirteen votes for acquittal of a baby killer, with only twelve jurors.

ETERNAL STONE
Majestic peaks, wrinkle and turn old
shedding rocks eager to roll with the cold,
sunshine adsorbing transmuted snow
destined for something, somewhere below.
Vagrant rocks will crash and crumble,
shake off their armor as they Tumble
seeking freedom in the mountain stream.
In waters, nacreous they gleam
with their drab exterior worn away.
Exposed, mute words they try to say.
about their strange tumultuous birth.
From volcanos and upheavals, Earth
spit out rock as melted magma chilled
in crystalized form, a destiny fulfilled.
Proud stone, will not keep its grain,
assaulted by wind or ice and sun or rain.
Downstream, rocks turn into stones and
then to pebbles, lastly to finest sand.
Did meekly broken rock know it was fated,

to be compacted, smelted and re-circulated,
yet rise again in another majestic peak,
when first it tumbled in the mountain's creek?

TWO BROTHERS

In the austerely white yet expensive Intensive Care Unit of Tampa General Hospital, Tom Druckman breathed sweet oxygen, turning his blood deep red. Tom dreamed a pleasant dream of triumph. Healthy blood cells drained of their poison, in a new and functioning kidney, streamed from his lungs carrying enough oxygen to nourish muscles atrophied during his two-year course of kidney failure. That supercharged blood sustained Tom as, in this healthier dream, he easily escaped from his older brother, Cliff.

This new surprise victory in an oft-repeated dream, also verified his triumph over death, despite his Doctor"s gloomy prognosis. Just yesterday, he had overheard Doctor Weldon say to his girl friend Marge, "Tom's body can no longer tolerate dialysis, and his vital organs are beginning to shut down. Better notify his close relatives that death is eminent."

When sick, Tom's tormented dream often revisited the same ugly incident when he had rebelled against his parent's practice of buying the new clothes for their favorite, older son, Cliff. Tom resented wearing clothes half worn out. Envious of Cliff's new 'Miami Dolphin's' warm up jacket, Tom had wet the sleeves and tied them in tight knots. When dried the Gordian knots had left permanent wrinkles.

Always before, in dreamed reprisals, his older brother caught him easily and repaid him for spoiling his favorite jacket by rubbing Tom's face in the dirt, pushing his nose flat against the ground, until Tom cried Uncle. That real life, but thirty year old surrender, still poisoned his feeling for Cliff.

Twenty years ago, it had taken almost a month of of after school, hard labor in the family's twenty acre truck garden to pay off the parental penalty imposed for the desecration of Cliff's jacket. The long, hot hours crawling on his knees, pulling weeds from raspy and chafing tomato plants. Worse still was working a whole a day to fill each discarded gallon sized sorghum pail with tomato cut worms and earning three lousy dollars credit toward his obligation. The gathering of a dozen pails full of repugnant cut worms also left Tom with lingering animosity toward his parents and all stoop labor. That forced compensation was compounded by the indignity of wearing that same mutilated garment for three years, while his brother brother proudly wore its replacement. Tom could see the incriminating wrinkles as long as he wore the jacket, although no one else could, and it took two years to outgrow the spoiled jacket.

The hate for his brother and lust for revenge outlasted the reviled jacket, but getting even had been less obvious than the knotted sleeves. First, sixteen year old Tom matched and then exceeded the size of his nineteen year old brother. His secret vendetta continued until he had won the ultimate revenge. Tom had wooed and won Marge, the first sweetheart of his more timid brother. Cliff lost that battle gracefully and never tried to replace his loss.

Tom awoke from his triumphant dream and snidely greeted, his lovely and patient companion, "You still here, Marge?"

"Hey Grouchy, are you back with us again?", she responded brightly, not showing one bit of fear or regret.

Tom never could find evidence of disappointment or surrender in her demeanor. All during the crisis that began when Tom's kidneys first failed, Marge had seemed upbeat. Sometimes with tears welling in her eyes, When he cruelly tried to drive her away and to a new life. "For a while yet, my dear," he said doing a poor and amateur imitation of Boris Karloff, then shifting to his customary whine, "Doc Weldon must still have kids, at home and can't spare the loss of another paying patient. By the way, how much of this week's billing will be covered by insurance?"

"What difference does it make if you don't intend to pay it, anyway?" Marge said warily, hoping her summation would not provoke another storm concerning their shared financial crisis.

Although Tom was apparently healthier, Marge, still tried to spare Tom the additional stress of considering their financial status. "Don't think of the money, Tom. Be glad to be alive. Cliff and I will find the money somewhere."

Tom interrupted, "Cliff and you ruined the only way we had to pay all the damned doctor bills. Over-claiming wages for more hours than the store was open, for instance."

Her usual of silence seemed admission of complicity or guilt over the failure of 'THE CHURN', but a healthier Tom deserved truth, and Marge complied, "The expense that killed your bottom line wasn't Cliff's wages. He never billed any overtime since you got sick,"

The brothers had jointly inherited their parent's successful ice cream store four years earlier, when their parents died in a tragic home fire. The retail ice cream store had been their parent's long-time dream and escape route from truck farm drudgery. It had been successful from the start and a happy workplace for the senior Druckmans. It should have provided well for their sons but it didn't. Tom blamed Cliff for the failure, and absolved himself because of his absence from the store when it finally closed.

Groping for the sympathy Marge usually brought to his bedside, George,s eyes focused ominously on his ICU monitor, to his left, then, more weakly answered,

"Cliff spent longer hours, at our store because he loved pigging out on ice cream. Not because the over-time was necessary. Cliff ate more ice cream than he sold. He abused his health, over-eating, yet his kidneys are fine. Our losses began when you quit running the cash register and kept the books at home! When the cats away, the mice will play."

Marge lost her composure and angrily replied, "So who started robbing the till, Sweetheart? All of the counter girls watched you skimming, so maybe a few did, but Cliff really watched them close and he set a good example. That's why he was there all the time. I still stopped by and closed both registers, every night. The register printout and cash were always close. Don't judge other's by yourself." Marge breathed a deep sigh, worrying that her explosion might trigger a relapse for her long pampered house-mate, but Tom had selective hearing and tuned out her complaints.

Unabashed, Tom continued, "Cliff needed watching. We made money, while I was there."

"I was there, and you didn't," Marge said unwilling to accept the half truth recollections previously tolerated during Tom's repeated hospitalizations, "You teased Cliff about his pudginess, until he wouldn't eat. You ate twice as much, but your heavy smoking kept you skinny and unhealthy."

"Baloney! Cliff was never tough enough on the counter girls. They had him wrapped around their finger. I made them work," Tom said smugly, while wanting the conversation to stop. Marge seemed different, today, not at all agreeable.

Tom struggled to erase the memory of their banker granting that first mortgage extension, but warning him that his gruffness did not inspire gracious manners in 'THE CHURN'S' serving staff. Discourteous service drove away most of the regular customers of the once popular and prosperous ice cream store. The banker had extended once, he said, because of their enviable location just off Tampa's Bayshore Boulevard where tourist and pedestrian traffic was heavy. That had been when Tom stopped blaming the location and began faulting Cliff. He repeated his current mantra; 'THE CHURN' began failing when Cliff took over management. It was too much for him to handle."

Marge exploded, "Look Buster, if you are finally getting better, you can face the truth. When you got sick and left, things did get worse, all right. Insurance rates tripled, and big brother government made us insure counter girls who worked more than twenty hours a week. Our total labor cost doubled."

"Our labor cost? When did you become a partner? You were exempt from bills, remember?" Tom said, but regretted immediately, and braced for Marge's outraged answer.

And his petite companion roared, "I thought I was part of the company because you didn't pay me wages, when you quit working! That stupidity was illegal and caused your last big argument with Cliff. He called you a cheap SOB!" "Well remember, I told Cliff to raise prices, first. I counted on his obvious affection for you to force him to increase prices," Tom meekly responded, with a new twist on that newly surfaced grievance.

"That too, Tom? You used me, all right. From the day we met," and Marge's sympathy continued to sour. She could feel her cheeks burning indignantly.

"Instead of wages, you had the use of allof my draw, Marge. Even though you mostly stayed at our apartment to work on the books."

"Why you ungrateful stinker, I didn't go to the store at all when you were awake. You are a taker, Tom. I waited on you incessantly. I was nominated giver, by you. I even had to draw out of my savings to keep you in food and medicine, and then be your cheery private nurse. Check the cost of home nurse care eighteen hours a day."

"You went out every night, Marge. I never asked to you sleep in the guestroom. How did I know where you were partying? I often pushed the buzzer and you did not answer or come..."

"Closing out the cash registers and talking to your brother, every night is not a party."

"I suppose he told you what a mistake you made dropping him, to come with me."

"He didn't have to tell me. I soon guessed the realy reason you chased after me, was because Cliff liked me. We only had one date, before I met you. He never called, after you asked me out, or we would've continued dating." Pensive, Marge momentarily stopped her assault.

Tom enjoyed the respite, remembering. The conquest of Marge and his victory over his older brother was somewhat hollow, as her appeal had diminished when the competition ended. He had convinced her to live together, rather than marrying immediately.

Marge resumed but quieter, and more careful with her words, "Cliff had a sympathetic ear and would listen to my problems and care. I heard his problems too. Never did figure out why we both were trying so hard to please you."

"Cliff's a sore loser! He chose to stay single because he lost his girl friend to his younger brother. I never talked you out of anything," Tom petulantly responded, while noticing his monitor tracing was reflecting the stress of their argument. He concentrated his gaze on that instrument, hoping Marge would notice too and decide her changed bedside manner was endangering him.

It didn't work. Marge continued her diatribe, dredging up another closeted ghost."Except the baby! I don"t think Cliff would have talked me out of having a baby, and he could afford a wife."

"I wanted a baby, Marge. I just wanted to wait until were married," Tom said with all the fervor of a self-appointed confessor.

"When did you ever ask me to marry?," she snapped, incredulously.

"I did want to get married, but so many things interfered." Thinking back, he had really needed Marge, but wasn.t ready to marry anyone. Seeing her increasing anger so long submerged, he tried again with in a penitent manner, "I planned to ask you the day you told me you were offered the promotion on your job, and just felt a little unworthy, of you and your success."

"It didn"t stop you from begging me to help you run 'THE CHURN', as if your Dad would trust you. I believed you and turned down my promotion, and I found you were just dreaming. Only when your folks died in the fire, did you have the right to make me a partner. Now, I realize that fire was damned convenient. Then you didn't because Cliff's full half, would top your diluted by marriage share, and you couldn't stand that."

"Marge, I had marketing experience, and Cliff did not. I didn't want him to ruin a family business that my folks had scrimped and slaved for all of their lives"

"You had marketing experience in a nothing job! You were aching for a reason to quit the meat counter. Cliff was a journeyman plumber and sure didn't need marketing experience", Marge said spitefully, daring an answer.

"Aw come on Marge, I was Assistant Manager of the whole meat department, and dealt with customers all the time. I was getting experience to get my own meat market."

"Why did I buy the groceries and pay the rent, Tom? I earned good money! Accountants move up into management. When, I was promoted, you begged me to stay and help you run the family business for half of what I was earning. Some choice..."

Wanting to stop recriminations, he attempted a summary confession, saying, "I've been a little jealous of Cliff. and blamed it all on my brother"s unfailing luck. He doesn't deserve good health, and I'd love to tell him..."

Marge interrupted, and asked, "Why don't you tell him to his face? He's here in the hospital anxious, to see you."

"Go get him," he bitterly responded, "If I can really pee, I want to do it first on Cliff".

Marge says, "You can, courtesy of Cliff. He foolishly chose to give you one of his healthy kidneys. Since you are not dying, you don't need me! I will undo a big mistake, I made. I am going to leave you and beg to marry your brother, Cliff. He may have only one kidney now, but he does have a much bigger and healthier heart. A heart that is compassionate and benevolent and is capable of love, and a love that I have needed, and missed too long."

Tom gasped hard but failed to breath air. The last sound he heard was the ICU alarm horn, sounding faintly from the nurses station down the hall.

Later, Doctor Weldon, attempted to console a guiltily grieving Marge, "Apparently Tom's heart was too damaged to handle any stress, and the operation was traumatic. Anything might have caused his fatal attack. Just remember your good times together and try to get on with your life."

WHIST ON DEATH ROW

Maynard sat up and swung his feet to the cold iron floor, achieving instant reality even on this humid August day. For six years, two months and twenty four days he had marveled at the constant coolness the boiler plate floor afforded, and on the very hottest days of August, he left the lumpy comfort of his corn shuck mattress, to shed body heat to the metal floor. The six o'clock wake-up horn had not yet sounded, and he wondered why. Even on this, his last day on Earth, he wanted the torture of his dreams instead of reality.

He was not alone. Someone sat on his commode, speaking in a eerily resonant, yet soft voice. "God sent me to help you, Maynard Whist."

Maynard had told the polite but steadfastly vindictive warden again yesterday that he did not want any sanctimonious, holy-rolling preachers trying to make him feel any worse or better than he did already, but few of his requests were recognized. Whist growled, "Whatcha you doing here. I told Warden Grimes, I didn't want no preaching. You and your prayers ain't gonna keep me from frying." Maynard guessed the strange man could be one of the death row guards who delighted in teasing Maynard, playing the game they called 'Whist on Death Row'.

"I'm here to help, 'cause you ain't got anyone else." The tall but stooped mysterious stranger sank from the commode to kneel much like Maynard's nightly prayer posture forcibly learned from the Evangels, one of his many frustrated foster parents. The stranger beckoned as if he expected Maynard to follow.

Patiently, the visitor began, "Hey, I'm not here to hear you beg. I'se here to help you die...."

"I learnt how to die along time ago, and the learn'n didn't come from no Saint or Preacher. Your wasting your time here!" Maynard said, hoping it was true. Maynard remembered learning how to die on his first stint in prison when he was raped by a sex-starved lifer who had abandoned female druthers. "No matter how bad, iffen it"s gonna happen anyway, don"t fight it," he said, echoing the words of that long ago ravager.

The stranger held out his hand, "If you will just trust me, death will be easy. The man can't hurt you no more."

Maynard defiantly held his hands up toward the stranger, "Do I look scared Look at these hands! Steady as a rock! I ain't a man needing prayer or forgiveness! Dying is easy, and ya only gots to do it once."

Soothingly, the stranger began, "Today is the last day you can tell the big man your sorry."

Maynard, irritated and sensing a meekness in his visitor, again interrupted, "Anyway, I shouldn't have to die. If that jerk, Johnson, had done me straight like I told him, steada trying to trick me with a rubber check, we'd both be better off. Hell, I knew he would just scream for the cops, iffen I took his check, no matter how hard he promised.. If he'd had some cash, I'da been out of his bedroom and he'd still be there sleep'n with his snoring wife. She almost saved herself, by just sleep'n so sound! Why the Hell could'n he let me just rippem off? It's his God damned fault he's dead, and I'm here wait'n to fry!"

Groping for his state issued, steel rimmed glasses parked on the floor, slowed his tirade enough for his dark clad caller to ask, "Were the Johnsons afraid?"

Confidently aware he was facing someone inquisitive, not an inquisitor, Maynard, decided to give him the real version of that long ago murder. Without self-pity or excuse, he began, "They screamed and begged, promised me their life's savings if I lettum live. Can you imagine, wanting to write me a check. The man said

-168-

he, would cash something called IRAs to make the check good."

Needing a moment to remember the real truth, he was patient when his new cell visitor asked, "If all's you wanted was their money, why not grab the check and scram?"

Maynard's memory of that bloody night was returning, and he was willing to share that recollection, speaking slowly as he carefully fitted the wire bows of his glasses over his ears, "They'd promise me anything, with a knife agin their throat. She couldda run, I couldn't kept em both with that little knife. It took so long to put him down but she would not leave. Just kept begging, 'Not my George, let him be', over and over, even when I started cutting her, It went so much quicker with her. She didn't get her hands in the way or fight. I guess that's why people that are gonna die, fold their hands and pray, to get em outta the way. Makes it easier for everybody."

The shadowed face of his caller seemed so familiar, and he seemed to be wearing an orange jump suit just like his. Even in the always lit 'killers row' the stranger seemed unfocused, even with glasses on. He leaned toward the mysterious stranger, who held up a commanding hand, saying, "You took their social security check. That's how they found you. Why take a traceable check? Did you want to be caught?"

Maynard explained, "I onliest agreed to take their social security check so they'd feel safe while I figgerd how I was gonna do them. Having them sign that check was how I got them both together without a struggle. They were a pray'n away, asking God, like I was gonna walk away. If I'da found any real money, I'da been outa there before they woke. Remember that! Keep some real money on hand. It could save your life when you get burglarized. I could've…I, I, I almost let'm live, like I almost believed em."

No longer resentful of his unperturbed visitor, Maynard listened almost courteously as his inquisitor sneered, "So how did that make you feel? Hearing em beg? Make you feel big?"

Surprised by his perception, Maynard confessed, "I Loved

hear'n em beg. It felt good. I felt in charge, for once. I felt rich, powerful. Everything they had sweated and saved for, they was trying to give me. I was better than them."

The stranger stood, placing a surprising hand on Maynard's left shoulder, explaining, "But only while they were alive and begging, weren't you sorry? Wouldn't you have wanted em..."

Sensing the sermon beginning, but feeling almost regretful, Whist admitted, "I guess I was afraid to listen longer...like maybe I'da done something foolish, let'm go or something. Maybe I was afraid they could fool me into trust'n em. Hey, I don't trust anyone." Persistently, his questioner probed, "You mean you were afraid you would feel pity for them?

"Are you trying to trick me into saying, I'm sorry?" Maynard sighed deeply, and then continued, "What's done is done! "I'd probably do it different, next time. Maybe, I'd take a rope to ty'em stedda kill'n 'em." Maynard hung his head, avoiding eye contact with the apparition that looked just like himself.

The stranger said, "Sooner or later, you'd take some poor soul's life. No way, you'd go back to prison, Right?"

"I ain't never been afraid to do time," Maynard confided as stared at the floor, "Done time all my life, and I turned fourteen in reform school. I wasted years, putting off the real ending. Sooner or later, I was gonna be here waiting for old sparky. The first time they lock you in the joint, they're starting to fry you. Dumb people like me, can't get no jobs worth anything. No damned wonder we get jealous of those who fit, and try to even up things. Box us up when we get caught, but don't teach us nothing so we can get a decent job, and a chance to make it outside the walls. The only teach'n we get is in the yard, scheming and dreaming on the perfect scam. We learn to hate the man, we learn to hate law. The law is the enemy and always looking to get you, we learn to hate anyone who fits in the right boxes. If you can't fix what put us in stir, if you can't re-cycle us like cans or waste paper, zap us the first time we get caught. It would be a whole lot cheaper, and kinder too. If you ain't got the stomach for sending men bound for prison, direct to old Sparky, you better turn your jails into fixit shops for twisted people, stead of cages where you teach us misfits how to hate the man. That first judge that sent me to prison killed the Johnsons, not me." Maynard's mantra was polished, from his years in prison.

After a moment of reflection, Maynard's visitor asked, "If you got the way for people to live together peaceably, tell me. Givers need protection from takers, the weak need to be protected from the strong."

For a few minutes, Maynard quietly thought, then responded, "Well I'd pair people up so's nobody get's nothing they don't want. Ain't nobody doing anything, that someone, somewhere, don't want done to them. Them as likes to kick the guy what's down ain't any sicker then those who like to get kicked. Like there's more people talk'n suicide than people who get killed. Every one should be able to get the things he needs without taking it from someone so greedy they got more'n they can use."

The stranger loomed taller and seemed concerned, asking, "Well, how would you make people do what is right? Would you let the mean and greedy live among and victimize the weak and needy? Would you send good fortune only to those who deserve it? Would you give blessings to those that did not ask?"

"Well, ain't praying just begging for something you can't get yourself, asking God for all'st you need?"

"So, why did you never ask God for help?"

Maynard bristled, "I ain't got no God, and iffen I was, I sure wouldn't come to this hell-hole."

Patiently, the stranger resumed, "You never asked God to come. Ya gotta ask, cuz no body should come helping or visiting if they ain't asked."

A wisp of epiphany brightened Maynard. He arrogantly proclaimed, "Well, Iff'n I wrote the rules, if I turned the cards, I'd do it face to face. How dare God write the rules but punish us like a sneak, not even looking his flunkeys in the eye. Only a mean boss would call in his dues before he'd set the terms. And iff'n a man's time comes to pay for something bad, I'd be there to tell why and what he's owing back."

Suddenly, feeling sorry for himself, he continued, If they is a God, he sure must be a shy Cuss! Any God running the whole shebang should show each man, woman and child that he's the boss. My only working job, I never, ever did see the Boss. Iff'n I had, looked him in the eye, I might not have stole from him. You know, if he'd said, `I won't keep anyone who takes my things. If I saw God, saw him face to face, heard the reward for living good, I might of tried to undo the bad I done folks that didn't deserve it, or tell the Johnsons I was sorry.!"

Maynard raised his head and stared at his accuser, seeing his face for the first time, recognizing now a strange similarity. Bathed golden by the now emerging dawn's first light, his caller's visage was so much like his own. Even a scar like the cigarette burn on his forehead. He must have stolen from his ma's purse, too. He demanded, who are you?"

He heard this visiting golden-self say, "Each man finds God, when in a mirror. Each man feeds the fire of his own Hell or pardons sin for Heaven's grace.

Regretful, not of his deed, but of his nearing death, Maynard's composure broke, and he whined, "Ain't no mercy for me, I know what you all wanna hear and I ain't gonna beg, or even say I'm sorry.

The visitor stepped back, and knelt again, beckoning Maynard to follow. "I forgive you, and God will listen…"

Sarcastically but willing for a miracle, Maynard pled, "Help me! You wanna help me, go sit on 'Old Sparky' for me. Take my place, go die for me!"

The unfamiliar visitor's image was fading but his voice resonated through Maynard's cell, "You have that kind of God!"

A new voice he recognized as the Warden's intruded, "Hey

Whist, the chaplain is here with me, and really wants to pray with you. The Governor has refused a stay so your execution is still scheduled for nine which leaves you an hour before we get ready."

Maynard Whist quickly spun from the impermeable barred door, toward his commode but sees nothing. He is alone.

ENVIRONMENTAL WARNING

If there be God, He must be miffed
        to witness mute, while man wild dare
        pollute their most essential gift,
        of seas creating clement air.
Will oceans, once with algae green,
        replenish air from seas, unclean?.

Would God be proud, that man has learned
        to squeeze the oil from ancient clay
        and fashion goods to earth returned
        as plastic trash that can't decay?
Will trees, our smoke makes weak and bare,
        no longer grow in poisoned air ?

If our Creator, we must please
        inventive man should soon take stock
        of chemicals that foul our seas,
        transforming Earth to lifeless rock.
Will Seals applaud the end of man
        who made their seas his garbage can?

We've changed this world to comfort zone
        without regard for any guest
        and think the world is ours alone,
        all life must serve at our behest.
Will someone care when man is gone?
        Not hunted deer or orphaned fawn.